Memphis Moon

TS Meeks

ISBN: 978-1724233783
Library of Congress Catalog Number:

Cover Art By:
Copyediting By: Keyoka Kinzy
Typeset By: Write on Promotions

Acknowledgement

To my best friends, who encouraged me to start this journey, Temu, Tricy, and Tamara, I love you! You told me I could do this exactly when I needed to hear it!

To my work family, who always asked, "Are you writing this weekend, you all pushed me through, so thank you!

To the amazing Dr. Carolyn R. Green, Aaron Jordan, and Ni'cola Mitchell, I couldn't have made this journey without you! Thank you for support it means the world to me!

Dedication

To my husband, thank you for your love and passion in all things. I love you!!!

To my children, you two are the stars that shine bright in my world. I love you!!!

Chapter One

It was September and beautiful in Memphis. I was on my way to the Liberty Bowl for some tailgating. My bestie, Charese, and I had to make a quick stop at the store. As I pulled into the parking lot, I saw the most beautiful man I had ever seen in my entire life. Charese told me to stop drooling and say something, but I couldn't move. I just stared. Suddenly, he started walking towards us. He looked at me and said, "You will be my wife," then walked away!

What in the hell had just happened? I watched him walk into the store, and Charese just laughed. I had to go find out what this guy on. We met in the center aisle, and he had the biggest smile on his face, as if he knew what I was about to say.

"Excuse me, sir," I said. "How are you going to claim me when I don't even know you? Are you a stalker?"

"No," he said, laughing. "I just saw you and knew you were the woman I needed in my life!"

I was so breathless. I thought I was going to pass out. He was tall, at least 6'4", and very handsome. He had hazel eyes and from what I could see, his body looked as if it was chiseled by the gods. *What a package!* He said his name was Kol Martin, and he walked me back to my car, promising to call me later. Charese wanted to know what happed to the snacks!

Later, Charese and I were talking about our plans for the weekend when my phone rang, and it was Kol. He wanted me to come over later to hang with out with him and his friends. He told me he was visiting from Chicago and was only in town for the infamous Southern Heritage Classic game between Jackson State and Tennessee State. It's the biggest party in September! Battle of the bands, the tailgating, food, people, and the live entertainment is out of the world. Nobody does a Classic like Memphis!

We haven't missed one in years! We plan for this day! Tents are everywhere and we wait in line to get the prime spot on Tiger Lane! You see everything and everyone from Tiger Lane! It's a must see!

At first, I wanted to go hang out with Kol, thinking what the worst that could happen is, but Charese reminded me that plenty could happen.

" You don't even know him," she said.

"For some reason, I just know I'll be ok with him," I told her "Besides, there's a locater on my phone. He'll give you his information." The plan felt solid and I felt like I would be safe with him. I didn't care and thought to myself: *live a little*. I was so tired of the Memphis dating scene.

Charese still didn't seem convinced, but I decided to go see Kol anyway. I had planned to go to Chicago in two weeks for our annual girl's trip anyway.

Once I met him, Kol and I talked for a while. We seemed to have so much in common and before I realized it, it was midnight. Kol was only going to be in Memphis for one more day, so we decided to spend it together. I blew off my plans with the girls that next day, and we did everything we could in those few hours. Since his plane didn't leave until 7:00 that night, we had all day. I took him around Memphis to see some of our most beautiful sites.

We went downtown to the Riverfront to enjoy the sun and took a quick tour on the Memphis Queen at Beale Street Landings. We visited the Slave Haven, the landmark home where hundreds of slaves crossed the Mississippi river through Memphis. Afterwards, we went to the Civil Rights Museum and walked through history! We had a great time, and I felt like I had known him forever.

The excitement was short-lived as soon the time came to bring Kol to the airport. His friends would be waiting. We loaded all his things in my car, so we could spend every second together. His friends were already at Memphis International. When it was time for him to leave, he asked for a kiss goodbye. I had wondered how long it would take for him to get to that point! When Kol kissed me, it was like nothing I had ever felt before, and I melted in his arms.

The way he held me was beautiful. His arms swirled around my waist. He was strong yet loving at the same time. When he let go, I felt like I was floating in a euphoric state! I was in pure lust and wanted more. I hadn't told him about my scheduled trip to Chicago because I really didn't know if I would want to see him again. After that kiss though, I had to tell him, in hopes that he would want to see me. Kol was happy with my news, or so it seemed, and he told me he couldn't wait to see me again! No one had ever had an impact on me like Kol did. I

3

slowly went back to my girls after his plane took off, needing something to lighten me up until I could speak to him again. The girls met me for a late dinner and drilled the crap out of me. They wanted to know everything about the day he and I had sent together. Damn, my friends were nosey! Charese and my other friends, Tammy and Lindsey, asked me so many questions that I couldn't get one answer one before the next question was asked.

Tammy probably already knew every turn we had made that day with her inspector gadget ass. She was more tech savvy than me, and I was good! I bet she even tracked me when I went to the bathroom! I told them I had never felt like this before, that whatever it was felt amazing. We were about to leave when my phone rang, and it was Kol! I lit up, so happy he had made it back to Chi-town safely. He told me he was still in the airport, but just had to call me. He said missed me already, and I just smiled.

I told him I was out with the squad, and he should go ahead home to get settled in. We'd have plenty of time to talk later. *Damn, he is good!* I thought. The girls and I went our separate ways, and I went home to wait on Kol's call. I had been home about an hour and hadn't heard from him. *He must be fucking his girlfriend by now,* I found myself wondering. *How could I be so stupid to get caught up with a man that I just met?* I tried to forget about that kiss at the airport, but I couldn't. I just kept seeing it repeatedly in my head and finally, I could feel it! I had lost it then. I knew I had to let it go.

I took a hot bath and put on some music, so I could get settled into the bed. Work would be calling in the morning. I got in bed and was about to fall asleep when my phone rang. It was Kol!

"Hi," I answered.

"My Sam, I have missed you," he said.

"You don't have to pretend anymore," I laughed. "You're home now, and the expectations are all gone."

"There aren't any expectations to keep up," Kol quickly responded. "I knew from the moment I saw you that this was real! You're the one for me."

"Hold up, too soon, too fast," I told him, but I was loving the attention. Kol had just told me I was the one! "Okay," I told him, "I'll play along since I'll see you soon, unless something changes."

We laughed and laughed for hours until I noticed it was one a.m.! I had to go to sleep because the office would not care if I was tired.

The problem was I was so wound up, I almost couldn't close my eyes. I replayed the entire day in my head until our last words. *What in the hell have I gotten myself into?* He was something else. I couldn't describe what I was feeling. The next morning, coffee and FedEx were waiting. My assistant, Lee, told me to spill. I ignored him at first.

"What are you talking about?" I asked.

"You're never this chipper in the morning, especially on a Monday! Who is he?"

"Lee, please just get my calendar for the day and more coffee."

When he returned, I was checking emails. "You have a call from the Marketing Manager at the AT&T office out of

Chicago," he said. "I didn't know we were working on something for marketing with AT&T. Did I miss a memo?"

"No, Lee, please put the call through." I waited for Lee to exit, then picked up my line. "Samantha Smith?"

"Good morning, My Sam. How are you? I miss you!"

"Kol, how in the world did you get my office number?"

"Sam, we run all of your office systems for telecommunications!"

"I said you were a stalker, Kol Martin!"

"Did I break any rules with you, Sam? If I did, I didn't mean to, and I hope I didn't upset you."

"No, silly, "I laughed.

"So," Kol asked, "how do you like them?" I was wondering what he was talking about, just as Lee walked in with a beautiful vase of red roses.

"Kol, you didn't?" I could hear his smile through the phone. "These are beautiful. You didn't have too."

"I know," he said, "but you are worth it and much, much more. I just wanted to make sure they made it, baby. I will call you later, Sam."

When I hung up the phone, Lee demanded answers right then and there.

"It's nothing serious," I said.

"I beg to differ, ma'am. No man sends long stemmed red roses for nothing."

I caved and explained to Lee what happened, how, and when. He was borderline in love too!

"Lee, you have to get out of my office. We have work to do today, you know!" I half-heartedly scolded. My day went by, and before I knew it, it was quitting time.

All I wanted to do was to talk to Kol. This went on for the next two weeks until Thursday night came around. I was trying to pack and talk at the same time. There was a call coming in, so I asked Kol to hold on. It was Charese.

"Hello, Sam. Yeah, the trip's cancelled."

"What? Wait, hold on!" I clicked over to Kol and told him I would call him back.

When I clicked back over to Charese, the rest of the squad was on the line.

"What in the hell happened?" I asked.

"Well, something work-related came up," Charese said.

"For me too, at Methodist. It was last minute," said Tammy.

"I'm still in," said Lindsey.

"I mean, I still want to go, but I don't want to go without the rest of the girls," she said. I was officially sad. I had to call Kol to let him know the trip we had been waiting on was a no-go. All my friends apologized. I told them it was ok, but I was heartbroken and doing an awful job hiding it. I guess it wasn't meant to be...

Once I hung up with them, I didn't want to make the call to Kol. Over the last couple of weeks, I felt like I had really gotten to know Kol, and I couldn't wait to see him. I waited and waited, hoping the girls would call me back to say it was just a cruel joke, but they didn't. I finally had to bite the bullet and call him.

When he answered, I couldn't hear the smile in his voice. "What's wrong?" he asked.

"Why would you ask that?"

Apparently, Kol knew me well enough to know that if everything had been ok, I would have called back much sooner.

"So, the trip is for sure cancelled. I won't be coming to Chicago after all," I told him. He paused, and for a moment, I wondered if he was still there. "Hello?" I prompted.

"The trip doesn't have to be cancelled. You can still come, Sam," he said.

"What?"

"Sam, I still want you to come. I still want to see you."

"Kol, the rooms have already been cancelled, and I would have to book something last minute. It's just too much, and maybe it's some kind of sign."

"Do you want to see me?" Kol asked.

"Of course, I want to see you."

"Then don't worry about it. Give me about 30 minutes, and I will call you back."

We hung up, and I wondered what was going on.

The next thing I knew, my email pinged with a new message, and my phone was ringing.

"You have flight leaving out tonight at 10:00 p.m.," Kol said. "I will be waiting for you when you land, and there's a room for you as well."

"Kol," I gasped, "this is a whole day earlier than I had planned. I can't do this. What have you done? I haven't even finished packing everything yet!"

"No worries," he said. "We can get everything you need when you get here. You know we do have stores here, too."

"You are crazy," I laughed. "I can't just up and leave like this."

"Why not?"

"I really hoped to get to know you better, Kol Martin, but I can't come alone. I have no information about you."

"Have you checked your email yet? No? Well, you should."

I jumped on my MacBook and checked my email. Kol had already emailed me the flight and hotel information, along with his driver's license, his insurance card, and his work I.D.

"Sam, how can you say no to me? Just get to the airport, and I won't take no for an answer."

"See, you are a stalker, just like I said."

He chuckled loudly. "Fine, fine. I'll be your stalker. Are you coming to see me or not?"

I thought about it again. *Live a little, right?* "What the hell," I told him. "I am on my way!"

On the way to the airport, I called the girls. They couldn't believe I was still going, and I couldn't believe it either. Earlier, I forwarded his email to them, so they knew where I'd be in case something happened. There I was, going to see Kol without any backup in the windy city. I only had time to pack an overnight bag, and I was sure I missed something.

9

When I got off the plane, Kol was there with red roses in his hand.

"I am so glad to see you," he said, giving me the biggest hug.

"You know this is crazy, right?" I replied, and he just laughed. When we found our way out of the airport, a Limo was waiting, and I was blown away. Kol was seriously trying to court me right now. I was overjoyed to see him, but I was trying to brush it off.

"Did you forward that email to your girls?" he asked.

"You know I did, so now they know you are a stalker, too!"

"That's fine by me. I'm just happy you came," Kol replied.

We had dinner at Fleming's Steakhouse, but had no idea what to do next. The connection between us was so strong, it wasn't hard to imagine what we could be doing. At that point, we had talked every day since we met, and it already felt like we were a couple. I just wasn't sure if I wanted to take the next step so early. I decided I was tired. It was time to go to bed and get some much-needed rest for the night.

The hotel suite was beautiful and again, a vase of long-stemmed red roses was waiting.

"Well," I said, "I guess it's time to say goodnight." I didn't really want him to, but it was the good girl thing to do.

"Wow, that was fast," Kol said with a smile.

"I mean, maybe you can come in for a little while...so we can talk."

"Okay, we'll talk."

"Yep, just talk," I repeated, and he laughed. Being a good girl is hard.

"Look, Sam, there's no pressure for anything. I could leave, if you want me to."

"Kol, I appreciate that. No, I don't want you to leave just yet. We're supposed to be getting to know each other," I said, calmer than I felt. *He was worried about pressuring me? That's funny.* There was enough pressure from myself for me to keep my hands off him.

We settled on the couch together and turned on the tube. The small talk came easily, but I wasn't paying attention to anything the tube had on. I'm not sure how it happened, but somehow, we had moved closer and our hands met each other. I needed to get away. I excused myself to the master bedroom. I knew I had to get it together, calm down, and breathe easily. When I came out after my pep talk, Kol was standing in the doorway. Our eyes locked, and without any hesitation, I just invited him to join me on the king size bed.

In response, he gave me the kiss I had been waiting for all evening. It was better than the first time, and I only wanted more. My fingers found his shirt and I gently pulled him towards the bed, but he stopped me.

"I don't want to pressure you into anything," he said.

"That's okay," I said, still breathless from our kiss. "Pressure away!"

He smiled and slowly laid me down. He touched me in places I didn't even know I had. In no time, I was ready to explode, and we were still fully clothed. Again, he stopped and looked into my eyes.

"We have plenty of time," he said. "This is real." He snuggled up next to me and held me tightly.

11

I felt safe and beautiful like I had never felt before. When the sun rose, Kol was still there next to me, holding me tight.

"Good morning," I breathed.

Kol kissed me on the forehead and said, "Hey, baby." That was the first time I thought I might be in love.

We got up for some much-needed coffee. As I shuffled through my suitcase, I realized that I would have to get to the store before long. I didn't bring a lot of clothes, but I just needed an extra pair of jeans. After a couple of quick showers, we headed for the store and to grab a quick bite to eat for breakfast. Before long, we went back to the suite.

"In a bit, I have to go home and change, too," Kol said, leaning in for a kiss.

"Well, you could also pack an overnight bag, too," I said, shyly.

"Are you sure?" he asked.

"Yeah, I want you to stay," I told him.

About two hours later, he was back, looking fine as ever. He told me I looked beautiful and I couldn't stop smiling. It was only the afternoon, but I wanted just a small taste.

Chapter Two

"You need something to wear tonight," Kol said suddenly. We were at Giordano's, enjoying some monster deep dish pizza.

"Why?" I asked. "What's tonight?"

"I made reservations at Sonya's," he said. "You'll love it Sam. There's low lights, great singers, and even better food."

"That sounds fun, but I'm on a weekend budget."

"No worries," he laughed. "This is my treat. It's my gift to you, Sam, for coming. I don't know how I would feel if you hadn't come this weekend."

Later, that night, we arrived at Sonya's and the atmosphere was very high. Everyone already knew Kol, and he was greeted warmly by the host. As we walked to our table, a few people nodded, said hello, and shook hands with Kol. I felt like a celebrity.

I just had to ask, "Do you come here often?"

"Sometimes," he answered, "when my girl is here for a set."

"Oh, your girl?"

"Sam, you're my girl," he said with a smile.

"Wow, you are really confident."

"What can I get for you, Mr. Martin?" the waiter asked. *Wow, he really must be a regular here.*

"I would like whatever Mrs. Martin would like," Kol said with a cheeky look on his face.

"What?" I balked.

"Yes, honey," he said. "You are picking the drinks tonight."

I smiled politely at the waiter and asked, "Could you give us a minute?" He nodded and scampered away, and I turned to Kol. "You are laying it on a little thick, aren't you? You added that Mrs. Martin for the flare, right?"

"Sam, I told you when we met two weeks ago that you were the one for me. I am just waiting on you to catch up." Well, I had nothing to say to that.

I skimmed the wine menu before beckoning the waiter over and Kol approved.

"See, I knew I could trust you," he said.

"It's just wine, Kol, not a car."

"Just wait, honey, you will get the chance to pick one out. This is just a little trial run of what you would do."

"Really? So, you are testing my skills?"

"Do you want to dance?"

"I guess I should show you what I can really do."

On stage, a woman crooned out Aretha Franklin's "Natural Woman," and I was on a high that was better than morphine. Kol looked into my eyes and said, "I hope you are ready."

"For what, Kol?"

"Ready to fall in love with me because it's happening right now," he answered.

Kol was right. I was falling somewhere, and I didn't care where it was.

When we were back in our seats, the waiter came back to take our order. I had the Asian Teriyaki Salmon, and Kol had the Grouper. We talked a bit, but the food was so amazing, we focused mainly on eating.

"Dinner was amazing, Kol. Thank you for this evening. I have really had a wonderful time," I gushed.

"Many more to come, baby. You will have it all, including me as a bonus."

"Really, you're the bonus? I can't wait to see what else I can get into then."

"That sounds like I should be calling for the check," he laughed.

"Oh, my goodness, Kol, what is on your mind?"

"Just you, Sam, you have been the only thing on my mind for the past two weeks. I have been waiting for this moment, and I couldn't have imagined it any better."

I was silent the entire ride back to the hotel. I couldn't stop thinking, *What was I going to do if he wanted to...*

"Sam," Kol's voice broke me out my thoughts. "We're here." I hadn't heard him and hoped he hadn't been calling my name for too long. "Sam? Where did you go?" he asked.

"Oh, I'm sorry I was just thinking." I got out of the car and follow him up to the suite. "Kol," I said suddenly, "I just want to tell you how much I have enjoyed this weekend. This beautiful suite and that dinner was amazing."

"Sam, this is nothing. Just wait until you realize I'm yours and you're mine. That's what's going to blow your mind."

"Kol —"

"Sam, if you really knew what I was feeling right now, you would be having an orgasm."

"Kol! You're coming on really strong."

"Look, baby, I can wait for you. That's not a problem, but there is no rule that says we can't have fun now," he said. I agreed. We went straight to the bedroom.

Kol laid me down on the bed. He began kissing my neck and running his fingertips up and down my side. "Is this okay?" he asked. "Should I stop?"

"No," I said, "Do whatever you want."

His erection was so evident, I couldn't miss it. Before we got to this place, I had imagined it was huge, but I didn't think it was as big as it felt. My mouth watered as he slid his shirt and pants off. His dick peeked out from his boxers.

"Are you sure this is okay?" he asked, as his lips brushed against my ear.

I pulled him close, as close as I could and gave in. "Kiss me," I moaned.

His lips were so soft and inviting. He sucked on my bottom lip before I invaded his mouth with my tongue. I managed to get out of my top quickly. Our tongues danced with each other in perfect rhythm. I ran my hands up his chest, feeling how solid this god-like body was. His hands ran down my stomach, and I realized I still had my skirt on.

Burying his head in my chest, his fingers found their way under my skirt to the inside of my thigh. I whispered soft incoherent things. I was out of my mind.

"Stop me, Sam," he said, "if you're not sure." I didn't. His fingertips trailed the lace on my panties until I felt his finger push inside! *Fuck*! I had never felt it like this before. It was just what I wanted, although his dick was thumping around all by itself. I reached down as he went in deeper.

Kol unzipped my skirt from the side and pulled it down as I wiggled under his grasp. With each pull of the fabric, he pushed his thumb on my clit hard. As I circled my hips, he circled his thumb, making me moan out with pleasure. I knew it was too soon, but I had to have him inside of me. I stroked his shoulders, down his arms, back up again, and I pulled him up for a hard kiss. As I pulled, I opened my legs for him, letting him know to go ahead and enter my dripping heat. He kissed my forehead and pulled out a foil packet that read extra-large! I bit my bottom lip as Kol traveled inside slowly. He went deep, deep, deeper… until I shook and trembled with pleasure. Kol touched my soul with his depth. He held me tight and caressed every inch of me. Then, he turned me over with little effort and kissed a trail down my neck, running his tongue down to the center of my back.

Kol was making me quiver and cry all at the same time. He had me so into him that I didn't want to ever let go. I wanted to fall asleep with his dick inside of me. *Oh God, how this man makes me feel…* I was dizzy from him twisting me around in positions, or was it euphoria? I was trying to rationalize what was happening. Every time he entered me, I only felt him marking me as his. He lifted my legs above his shoulders, making sure he got to the bottom of my love, pushing in as I moaned with unbridled pleasure. He rocked me forward, and I was sprawled on top of him. With one pump up, my eyes opened wide, and I sat up on his beautiful stick.

I was no longer in control of my body. My hips moved without permission.

"Sam, please," Kol groaned. "Please ride me, baby. Ride me good!" On command, I did, motioning my hips to his beat. I arched my back to push every bit of him inside me. Kol sat up in the middle, holding me tight and with that single, move my walls tightened around him. I was hot, and the impending explosion was about to shake me to my core.

"Kol, I'm coming! Oh God, I'm coming!"

"Sam! Come for me, baby!" I did and couldn't stop it if I wanted to. He gritted his teeth, pressing into my neck. "Shit, Sam, I am coming with you, baby!" I could feel his seed spilling out hot cum inside the rubber.

I fell off him onto the sheets, almost spent.

"I want you to always be mine, Sam," he said. I was searching for something to say, but he told me I didn't have to say anything. He just wanted me to know. I rolled over with what little strength I still had.

"We are moving too fast," I said. "I know what we just did was very special. It was like nothing I have every felt before, but –"

"Do you think I just make love like that on a regular?" he interrupted.

"I don't know your sex well enough to say, Kol," I said before I could stop myself. "I'm sorry. I didn't mean… Kol, we are just getting to know each other." I knew I had hurt his feelings and wanted to take it back because it hurt me too. "Kol I am trying not to like you so much. This is so new, and right now, it's like I can't control myself with you."

He got up without a word and went into the bathroom. I could hear the water running. *Shit, I must have really upset him. What am I going to do?*

"Come on in, babe," Kol called, peaking out.

The water in the bath was for me! God, where had that man been all my life, and how did I luck up on his dick?

The next morning, I got up earlier than usual to make coffee, and Kol was gone! I couldn't believe that after the night we had just had, he would leave. I felt so stupid. *Well Sam, you gave it away like a Christmas gift*, I said to myself. It was wrapped up in lace with a pretty bow! He got me. I felt like a hooker, but a damn good one.

I turned on Pandora. Brian McKnight's "Could" was playing. *Shit!* It was like a sign. I hopped in the shower and stayed there until the water ran cold. I still felt Kol inside me, touching me, kissing me, and I lost myself for a moment. I finished and wrapped myself in one of the plush towels, feeling empty.

I decided to pack up and leave early. There was no reason to stay. I started looking for flights that left that day. They would kill my pocket, but I couldn't stay. Just as I was about to book the flight, Kol walks through the door!

"Where did you come from?" I asked.

"I went by my mom's," he answered.

"Kol, I thought you left."

"No, silly, I would never leave you. I love you. I am just waiting on you to catch up, Sam."

"Kol, how could you possibly love me? You don't even know me."

"Sam, trust me on this one. I have been with you every day for the last two weeks, and this weekend, we have gotten closer. I know you feel it, so stop denying it," he said. I was speechless because he was telling the truth. I felt like I could give myself to him, and so I did. He had me, what could I say?

It was my last day in town. I was scheduled to leave on the 2 p.m. flight, so I could get home and rest before work on Monday. We took it easy with a light lunch. There were so many feelings circling around in me that left me uncertain. All too soon, it was time to get to the airport. We got there early, so we could sit for a while before I had to go through security.

"Kol, this weekend couldn't have been any better," I told him. "Everything was wonderful."

"Sam, just get use to this because you are my one."

"Flight 110 for Memphis will board," someone said over the intercom. That was it. I had to go.

"Will you call me as soon as you land?" Kol asked, holding me close. He kissed me goodbye and I left.

It occurred to me that I was leaving the first man I had ever truly fallen in love with. When I hit the ground, I couldn't wait to call Kol.

The phone barely rang twice before he answered. I could hear the smile in his voice. "I'm glad you made it home safely, my love, but I miss you already."

"Ditto," I replied and couldn't help myself from smiling too. Before I could get out another word, the girls spotted me. They were impatiently waiting for me to dish. "Baby, can I call you back?"

"Yes, my love," Kol said before hanging up.

"Damn," I said. "I just got here, Charese."

"Yes, but you didn't answer your phone the entire time you were there," Charese said.

"That's because she was being nasty," Lindsey said.

"You damn right, and I can't wait to do it again," I replied.

"Do you think you're in love with him?" Tammy wanted to know. "You gave him your cookies, didn't you?"

"Sorry, ladies. I have to get home," I told them. "Kol will be calling soon, and I don't want to miss his call."

Charese was stunned. "You do have your cell on you," she said. "He knows you made it here already because he probably activated the GPS tracker on your phone."

"Shade, Charese," I laughed. "Just so you know, I don't give a damn what he puts on me, as long as he puts it on me again."

I had to admit it. I wanted to call him on my way home, but I had to get myself together. I wanted to give him some space. Well, that's the lie I told myself. I promised the girls we would meet for lunch tomorrow, and I would tell them all the sordid details. I was just hoping I would be able to get through it without having an orgasm. I went home and unpacked first. I tried to keep busy until finally, I couldn't take it and called.

I could hear Kol smiling when he answered the phone. "Baby," he said, "I have been waiting on your call. How was your flight?"

"It was fine. I know I already thanked you for everything you did to me— I mean, did *for* me."

"Anything for you, girl," he said. I felt like I was back at Whitehaven High when a sophomore and one of the seniors liked me. "Sam, when are you coming back to see me?"

"Don't you want a break from me?" I asked.

"No, I can come to you if that's better."

I just laughed. We talked for hours and all too soon, I realized how late it was. He and I both had work in the morning but saying goodbye just didn't feel right.

"I will give you a call in the morning on the way into work, if that's ok?" he asked, uncertainly.

"I wouldn't have it any other way," I answered with a smile.

"Sam, if you can't sleep, or if you're restless for any reason, you can call me, no matter what time it is. I am yours."

Once again, I had nothing to say to that, but... "Goodnight, Kol."

It was morning. I got into the shower with music because that's just what I do, and I only heard love songs. I was thinking of Kol, seeing him, feeling him. I was doing just what he said: I was falling in love with him! I couldn't take it anymore; I had to call.

"Good morning, Mr. Martin."

"Good morning, Mrs. Martin."

"Kol!"

"What, my love? How are you this morning? I know you look beautiful. Hey, at lunch, will you facetime me, so I can see for myself?"

"Yes, Kol, I will."

"Do you know how good that sounds coming from those lips?"

"Stop it, Kol. I will call you later, love."

"Sam?"

"Yes, Kol?"

"Did you just hear yourself? You called me 'love,' and now it begins for you. I love you Sam, and I will see you later."

What in the world was I doing? It was a long day, or so it seemed. I couldn't concentrate on anything. It was lunchtime when I called Kol again, and it sounded like he was waiting.

"Babe how is your day going?" I asked when his face appeared on the screen.

"Sam," he said, "Do you realize you are using terms of endearment when you are speaking with me. Do you do know what that means? You are allowing yourself to love me."

"Kol, stop it."

"You know, I had a problem this morning, Sam."

"What was it?" I asked.

"You weren't in my arms when I woke up. Sam, that didn't sit well with me at all."

"I guess we will just have to work on that," I said, jokingly.

"Maybe we can meet for dinner tomorrow to discuss it. What time is good for you, Sam? 6:00?"

"It may be later than that. I haven't seen my mom since I've been home, and I want to go check on her. I will call you once I settle in ok?"

"Sure, Sam. I will talk to you later, my love."

I was home, already showered and in bed. Although I had a great time seeing mom, Kol kept sneaking up in my thoughts. Those days and nights with him had spoiled me. I wanted to feel him close to me again. I looked over at the clock. It was

11:15 p.m., and Kol was probably in bed. I was about to pick the phone up when it rang, and I was so happy.

"Hey, baby," I answered.

"Oh, I'm your baby now?" he asked.

"If you wanna be," I said slyly.

"I couldn't settle down, Sam. I miss you too much." I was melting. We talked for a while, then he told me he wanted me to rest.

"Well, okay," I said, a little sad.

"Hey, did you forget?" Kol asked.

"Forget what?"

"Don't forget I love you, and you will be my wife. I told you that over two weeks ago, so I thought this is a great time to remind you."

I sighed and said, "I won't, stalker." We both said our goodnights, and I fell asleep fast.

The next morning, I woke up looking for him. I had dreamed of him the night before and thought he was there with me. I couldn't get ready fast enough because I wanted to talk to him. As soon as I buckled up in the car, the Bluetooth was dialing.

"Hey baby, are you running late? I have been waiting on your call," he said.

"I am right on time, Kol, and I missed you," I said.

"Sam, I was wondering...have you planned your vacation already?"

"No, I haven't scheduled anything for the rest of the year. Why?"

"I want to spend Christmas with you."

"It's the beginning of October, and you are already planning Christmas?" I asked in disbelief.

"Yes, Sam, actually I am planning the rest of our lives," he answered.

"Are you serious?"

"Yes, you are the one."

"Kol, you love making me blush early in the morning!"

"That's not all I like to make you to do in the morning."

"I have to get in the office," I said, embarrassed. "I will call you later, once I get home."

"No lunch time call today?"

"No, the girls are on red alert," I explained. "They're waiting to hear about my trip since I blew them off yesterday."

"Well, make sure you tell them you loved everything I did to you," he chuckled, poking fun. "I mean, *for* you. I don't want the girls thinking I didn't take care of you while you were away from home."

"Kol, if I told them how well you did, you would have to round up about three brothers for them. Wait, do you have 3 brothers? No, don't answer that. I will find out later."

The morning passed in a blur and before I knew it, it was lunchtime. I was surrounded by my girls, being grilled with their questions.

"What do you see in him?" Charese asked. Everyone's head turned with a gush of air, shaking their heads.

"You were there with me when we met. Didn't you see him?" I rebutted.

"Yes, I did, Sam, but you have gone crazy over one weekend," she countered.

"Yeah, I have," I said simply.

"What's the problem, Charese?" Lindsey wanted to know. "If Sam's having fun, then let her have at it."

"Well," started Tammy, who hadn't said much all afternoon, "I think it's sweet. I mean, it's kind of adventurous that things are happening so fast. I think you should enjoy it for however long it lasts."

"We all should be enjoying our lives," said Lindsey, "and Sam, if Kol makes you beam like this, I am for it!"

"Thanks, girls. I love you," I beamed and threw an arm around Charese. "Girl, if you want to know so badly what about him drives me crazy, just come with me on the next trip."

She raised an eyebrow. "And when will that be?"

"In two weeks!" I shouted.

"Damn," she said, "he has got to have a monster down there if you are already going back!" We all broke out in a fit of laughs and spent the rest of my lunch gossiping.

When I returned to my office, I almost bumped into Lee, who was just leaving it. He crossed his arms with a cheeky grin on his face and said, "He's struck again." I laughed and swatted him on the arm.

"Kol, thank you for the flowers," I gushed the second he answered.

"You're welcome, love," he said and again, I heard the smile in his voice.

"Okay, now, I need to get off the phone and do actual work today, or it's going to be a disaster."

"Okay, love. Thanks for calling," he chuckled.

I fell back into my chair. What in the world was I going to do? I was falling in love faster and faster.

The day ended, and I called Charese as soon as I got in my car.

"Can I stop by?" I asked her. "I need to talk to you."

"Of course, Sam. Is everything alright?"

"Yes, I just need a sit down."

Chapter Three

I told Charese, and only her, that I was falling in love with Kol. I couldn't stop myself. She looked at me for a second, stared!

"Sam," she said, "are you sure you just haven't been taken in by his obviously big dick?"

"No, it's not that at all – although he is gifted, but seriously, Charese, what am I going to do?"

"Shit, I don't know. You are playing right? This is a joke! You have never been like this before about anyone, not even…"

"Don't you dare say his name. This is nothing like that, Charese!"

"I mean, I don't know what to tell you. We always come to you when we have man problems, but you never need advice from anyone."

"That's not helpful, Charese. I just don't understand myself. I mean, I have no idea what is going on with me right now. I think he is everything I want right now in my life, but I am so lost. I have no idea what I am doing; I just know what I am feeling, and it feels like love."

"That's ok, Sam. You can't know all the answers this early. Look, I'll go with you to Chicago in two weeks."

I was elated. "Charese, really? You'll come with me?"

"Of course, I want to see what this man is all about."

"Okay, I'll just make sure he doesn't mind a plus one."

"He better not," she said and made a face.

Later that night, I called Kol and asked if he minded if Charese tagged along. Of course, he didn't. "Anything that will make you happy," he said, "I want to do it ten times over."

The two weeks rolled around before we knew it, and it was time to go the Chi! We boarded the plane, and it seemed like right when we were about to start talking *Power*, the plane began to descend.

I couldn't wait to see Kol, but to my surprise, he wasn't there. I spotted a driver, who I know was waiting for us because his sign read: *Mrs. Kol Martin and guest.*

"Kol, what is going on?" I asked him the second he answered the phone. "The driver is here with a sign?"

"I know, baby, just get in the car," he said.

"It's nice to see you again, Mrs. Martin," said the driver. "I will be taking you and your guest to Mr. Martin's location." Charese was as stunned as I was!

We pulled up in front of a beautiful house with a white picket fence and flowers everywhere. I wanted to know where was Aunt B from Mayberry? The driver began taking our luggage out of the trunk.

"Where are we?" Charese asked.

"I have no clue. I've never been here," I answered.

"Will you ladies follow me?" the driver asked. We followed the driver and saw a sign labeling the place as a bed and breakfast, but there was no one else there! The owner wasn't even there!

"Kol!" I yelled as soon as we entered the B&B. "Where are you?"

"Right here, baby!" he shouted back. He came over and kissed me, holding me in his arms tight. I almost forgot Charese was standing there. I broke the kiss, a little embarrassed.

"Kol, do you remember Charese?" I asked.

"Of course, how are you?" he greeted.

"I'm good now," Charese said. "What are we doing tonight?"

"I have a few things lined up for us," Kol said.

"How come we just didn't get a hotel?" I asked, wrapping my arms around him. "Or better yet, your house?"

"I didn't want Charese to be uncomfortable," he answered. Charese smiled gratefully, and I almost squealed. This was a good start. "Come on, I'll take you ladies on a tour."

The den was just beautiful. There was a fireplace and tall windows draped in the most intricate linen. The bedrooms were so big, and they had fireplaces inside. It was so cozy, just the right place to make love repeatedly. Damn, I really did love this man, but I wouldn't dare say it out loud.

When he finished showing us around, Charese got settled into one of the rooms and we headed to the kitchen. I made a drink and stared staring at Kol.

"Why did you tell the driver I was Mrs. Martin?" I asked.

"Because you are. You're the only one that doesn't know it," he answered.

I rolled my eyes, let the drink slide down my throat, and found myself thinking: *I know it, but I won't tell you.*

Out of nowhere, Charese popped into the kitchen. "Ok," she said, "We had the tour, so when are we going to have some fun?"

I looked at Kol and said, "You wanted this one coming. I knew what I was getting into, but you?"

"I have something planned," Kol answered. "I reserved a club for us and invited a few friends and family." Okay, so I was meeting his people. That's a nice change. The last time I was in town, I only saw the top of the ceiling, bottom of the floor, and sides of the walls.

Oh weeeeee! So, we hit the town, and man, did we hit it. We went bar hopping for about an hour before heading off to the club he told us about earlier. We rolled up to the valet and were escorted in through a VIP entrance.

"Who in the hell is he connected to, Sam?" Charese whispered in my ear. Before I could answer, she asked, "Who gives a shit? I am ready to kick it!" Kol had reserved a whole section for us and his friends, who were already waiting.

"What's up?" Kol greeted everyone. Charese and I said our hellos.

"So, this is her?" one of the guys asked.

"Yeah, this is Mrs. Kol Martin and her girl, Charese. Ladies, these are my friends from way back, Eddie and Gene."

After talking for a while, I got the gist of who Kol's friends were. Apparently, Gene was well off, and Eddie was a hustler (and good at it). Kol ordered drinks and food for us. That was when all the fun started!

When I looked around, I notice that we were the only people on the entire floor. The girls on another level made it no secret that they wanted to join us. One of them sent up a bottle of Pure White Hennessey for Kol to enjoy.

"Friends of yours?" I asked.

"I only want you, Sam. I'm your number one fan," he said.

Goosebumps were everywhere. We got to know his friends. Charese was really enjoying herself. Every song was her jam! After a while, she and Gene went to a quiet spot when she wasn't dancing. It was so much fun.

Suddenly, the lights changed. "This is a special request from our very own, Kol Martin," the DJ said. It was Brian McKnight's "Could." Tears started to form in my eyes.

"Sam, I love you," Kol said, "and I will tell the world. You are Mrs. Martin!"

"Yes, I am!" I cried.

After hours of hanging out, we finally went back to the B&B. Damn, I couldn't wait to see what new tricks he had up his sleeve. We told Charese, Gene, and the others not to stay up too late and that we would catch them later in the a.m.

We got upstairs to our room. The lights were deemed, and the room was filled with candles, roses, and champagne. Jazz played softly in the background.

"Welcome to a night you'll never forget. Why don't you go take a nice bath and get ready for me?"

"Alone?" I asked.

"I have a few things in there waiting for just you." *When did he have time to do this?* We had been together the entire day and night. It was just unbelievable!

Everything was beautiful, especially him. He told me to take all the time I needed, and that he would go to the other bath. He kissed me slowly, like it was the first time. I was a little disappointed he wanted to separate and meet up later. I wanted him right then and there. I only said okay because I didn't want him to know how big of a slut I wanted to be. When I got out of my bath, Kol was waiting for me on the bed with drinks, strawberries, and chocolate.

Good God, I was in love! He gave me a glass. I stared into it so hard because with the way he was acting I knew there was a ring in it. To my surprise, there wasn't! Kol wanted to dive into a conversation about serious things, like where would I be in five years and how many kids did I want? It was intense and not at all what I wanted to be doing at that time.

"What are you leading up too?" I asked him suddenly.

"These are the things I need to know before we get married," he answered.

"What in the hell are you talking about?" I asked. "Kol, you are moving way too fast. I love the attention, but..."

"But what?" he asked. "I know you love me; I can tell by the way you look at me, the way you touch me, the way you make love to me. This is no ordinary love! This is real. I am not rushing you for anything. You can take your time, but you are her, the one I love and want to spend the rest of my life with."

"The rest of your life? That's such a long time, Kol."

"Sam, tell me you don't love me, and I will stop right now. Can you really tell me that?"

"I don't know."

33

"I know! I can feel it with every breath you take, just admit it."

I looked into his eyes. "Kol, I can't lie to you, I do love you."

"He kissed me and said, "That's all I want right now. Everything else will fall right into place."

The hugging and kissing and everything else came and it was still more than I could imagine. He put me to sleep the right way.

The next morning, I woke up and stretched my arms wide to find that Kol was missing again. *Damn.* I rubbed my eyes and felt something hard against my face. I looked at my hands. There was a ring that had to be about 5 carats on my finger.

"Kol!" I called. "Kol! Where are you?"

Charese barged in. "What the hell is wrong with you?" she asked. "Sam, do you know how loud you are?"

"Look at this shit, Charese!" I yelled. "Have you seen him this morning?" I asked in a normal voice. "Where is he? Charese didn't give a damn; she just stared at my hand.

"You hooked one this time, Sam," she said. I started yelling for Kol again!

"Yes, baby, what's wrong with you?" Kol called.

"Come here!" I screamed.

Charese was still standing there, smiling with her color commentary! "I love it, Kol," she said. "I will give you two sometime, but I will be back later!"

"What is it, baby?" Kol asked as he entered the room.

"What the hell is this, Kol?"

"What are you talking about?"

34

"You can't be serious!"

"Well, you sounded serious with all the yelling you were doing."

"What is this?"

"What do you think it is?"

I was breathing so hard I thought I was going to pass out.

"Sam, calm down. I told you that I loved you, and I meant it. I know this is fast, and I know you want to take it slow," Kol said. "I am not rushing you at all; I just want you to know that I am truly in love with you."

"What in the world am I supposed to say to this?"

"I don't know, Sam, but say something."

"I have been trying to not love you," I told him, my voice cracking. "I tried not to feel too close to you, tried not to think of you every moment of the day, but I can't! I am so in love with you that it's unreal. I wonder if I'm I crazy, if I'm in this long dream?" Once I started, I couldn't stop. I told him everything.

"I love you so much," I said, "so much that when I'm away from you, I ache. I can close my eyes and feel you wrapped around me. I fall asleep and dream of you and everything we have done from the first moment we met. I can't deny it anymore. I am in love with you, Mr. Kol Martin, now will you say something?"

I dropped my head. He lifted it back up and kissed me with so much passion I just knew my clothes would fall off!

"I am so happy, Sam," he said. "You have made me the most grateful man alive. I have been praying that God would allow you to see how much you mean to me and know that this is real. I love you with fiber of my being; my soul smiles from the inside every time I think of you and me. My heart skips every time I think of your smile. I love you, Sam, for today, tomorrow, and forever!"

That was the most wonderful day of my life. I was really in love! We began to make love, and this time it was different; it was spiritual.

We became one. The foreplay was so amazing. He made me scream. The way he held me, touched me was like nothing I had ever felt before. He kissed my body, sexed it, and caressed it. He took me higher and higher. I held onto him as he lifted me up and laid me against the wall. I felt his love go in and out, walking me over to the bed and not slipping out. He pushed my legs back against the headboard and spread them wide. He pounded in my love, giving me pleasure beyond words!

I rolled over, slowly loving all over him. I moved in all directions, making sure I felt every inch of him. I craved him, needing him to touch my bottom. I turned around and laid my face on his legs, putting my ass was in his face. I leaned back into his chest. He turned my head around to kiss me. I just knew this love was for the ages and not to be tried unless we were sure we wanted to give it all away.

Kol flipped me over, pulled my ass to his waist, and squeezed my thighs. He put every inch of himself inside me, whispering how much he loved me. He reached beneath me, and his thumb rubbed hard against my clit. My hands were gripping the sides of the bed tightly. I put my face in the pillow and moaned. Every inch of him inside of me dug deeper and deeper. I wanted to run, but I couldn't. He smacked me on my ass, gripping it tighter and tighter.

I felt how close he was to coming inside of me, but it was me who came all over him… the ultimate release. My love shot out, and he waited until I was completely empty before he released himself. His dick was throbbing, and he held me on my shoulders so tight. His love was now completely mine.

We cleaned up and finally went downstairs. Charese was waiting.

"Do you love her?" she asked before he could even sit down. "Do you love her enough to never hurt her, to always make her happy, and only have her cry tears of joy?"

"Charese," Kol answered, "You don't have to worry. I love her." He kissed me on the forehead. "I'll let you two have some time alone. I have some things to take care of." He reached inside of his wallet and gave me his credit card. "Have a good time, go get manicures and pedicures, whatever you want to do. The mall isn't far from here. Call me if you need anything."

"I love you, Kol," I told him.

"I love you, Sam."

"Are you all crazy?" Charese asked.

"No, Charese," Kol answered, "and get whatever you want, too. You are the closest thing to a sister Sam has, so to love her is to love you too. Enjoy your day."

Charese whipped out here phone before the door closed. "Lindsey," she said into the phone, "conference call! Get Tammy on the line and call me right back!"

"What the heck is going on?" Lindsey asked.

"You will find out in a minute," Charese said. "Now get to it." I just sat there in awe.

Two minutes later, Lindsey, Tammy, and Charese were all on speaker phone.

"What is going on?" Tammy asked.

"He loves her," Charese sung into the phone. "He loves her!"

Everybody started screaming. When they calmed down, Charese started to tell them everything happened, and they all were like school girls all over again. I was smiling so hard; it was an amazing feeling. The girls stayed on the phone for a little bit; I told them I had to get ready to enjoy this day.

"Where?" they asked.

"Oh, I forgot to tell you," Charese chimed right in. "Kol is sending us to the spa. I see why she loves him now. It's the way he tends to her that's unbelievable. I have never seen anything like this before. Oh, and – can I tell them?" she stopped to ask me.

"Tell us what?" they shouted.

"Might as well," I caved.

"He gave her a huge ring!" Charese screamed. I thought the roof was going to blow off! I just started laughing. I was in a place I had never been before. I realized for the first time, Kol was my soulmate.

I finally released from the girl squad to get ready. I sang the entire time, love songs, of course. We went to the spa and got the works. I felt so good, and I wanted to look good for Kol later. We did some minor shopping. I didn't want to go crazy with his card. We went to lunch and back to the B&B.

When we got back, Kol, Gene, and Eddie were there. "What's up, guys?" I greeted. They all just looked at me. "Did I do something wrong?"

"No, baby," Kol said, "they are staring because you are the most beautiful woman in the world, and I just told them how I feel about you."

"You must be something special," Gene said. "I have known him for a long time. I have met his friends before, but he has never been like this."

"Yeah, this is some strange shit for us," said Eddie. I went over to Kol and sat next to him. Charese sat across from Gene, looking weird.

"We've seen Kol in love before, or so we thought, until you, Sam. He is a good guy and treats all women with respect, but he has never described a woman the way he describes you," Eddie said.

"Congratulations," Gene said. I was in pure amazement. What man explains this to his boys, of all people?

I knew then that he was the one I wanted to be with forever. This was the love of my life! So, after all the craziness was over, we were ready to hit the clubs again. We went upstairs, and I made it known Kol and I should get one in.

"Everyone's downstairs," Kol said.

"I don't care," I whined. "They all know about us, and everyone is grown, so how about it?"

He looked at me. Damn, I love you!"

He kissed me, and I was heated. With every kiss down my body, Kol muttered: I love you, I love you, I love you! Even his sweat tasted good! We were so close, we could have been the same person What a man!

When we finally made our way down the stairs, Charese was tapping her foot like a mad woman.

"Good Lawd, did yall forget we were here? That's what it sounded like!"

"What do you mean?" I asked.

"I guess, yall couldn't help yourselves, huh?"

Kol and I just looked at each other, then at her. "Sorry," we both said with a shrug.

Chapter Four

We went to the club and once again, we had a section to ourselves. This time, a few more people were already there.

"Are all of these people with you?" I asked Kol.

"No, they are with *us*," he answered.

"With us? Who are they?"

"This is my family These are my sisters and brothers. You will meet mom tomorrow for breakfast."

"Kol, why didn't you tell me?" I asked, suddenly feeling scared. Eddie and Gene were right there, hugging, laughing, making themselves at home.

"How many of you Martins are there?" Charese asked.

Well, just these ten… that I know of," Kol said with a laugh.

"What? You're kidding, right?"

"No, my dad was busy with and *without* my mom. We all love each other no matter what my dad did to get us here. We don't blame anyone for it, so I hope you are ready because this will be some funny shit!"

I started making my rounds. The first sister I met was Candice, and I knew right off we would be cool. It seemed to go on forever, but it was so much fun to meet his family.

We laughed, danced, talked, and ate. It was a great night.

Charese pulled me to the side. "Let's go to the ladies' room," she said. We excused ourselves and went off to the bathroom. "Sam, I just wanted to say that I get it now. Kol is wonderful."

"So, you changed your mind?" I asked.

"Yes, any man that would put up with me and bring his whole family out to meet you must love you!" We hugged and went back to the section.

When we walked back in, I noticed there was a girl staring at Kol. I tapped him on the shoulder and asked, "Who was she?"

"She's someone from my past," he told me.

"Well, that doesn't feel right to me. What do you think she wants?"

"Baby, I don't care what she wants. I am all about us." Suddenly, Kol stood up and walked over to the woman, pulling me along. "Can you leave?" he asked the woman. "You're making my wife uncomfortable."

"Your wife!" the woman screamed. Everyone stopped moving.

"Look, Alisha, I don't want to argue with you," Kol said. "It has been over for so long. Why don't you just give up? We will never be together again."

The woman known as Alisha looked at me and asked, "So you are the new girl? Well, this won't last. He will be back before long, so have fun while you can."

"Kol loves me," I told her. "That's it!"

Candice came over to where we were standing. "Heifer, just leave," Candice said. "No one wants you here! Kol doesn't love yo' dumb ass; you are just in denial. Stay away from my brother, I mean it."

"Well, damn, Candice, so you are taken in by this new bitch, too?"

"What the hell did you just call me?" I asked her. I got up close and personal with her.

"Don't worry about her, Sam," Kol said.

"I'm not, but I got this," I told him. I moved even closer to her. "Look, Alisha, it's Alisha, right? This shit you are pulling right now is childish and ignorant. You may still love him, and trust me, I understand why, but you are not the one. I am with him now, and you will not disrespect him or me. This man right here loves me, and I am in love with him. Now, I am trying to be a lady, but don't get it twisted. Do you even know what that means?

"That means that I will not allow him to feel any pain, hurt, or anger. I will feel it for him. He means the world to me, and if you think, you can just come in and turn our world upside down, you are mistaken. Now, he asked you nicely because he is a gentleman, but bitch, I am not him, so get yo' ass out now!"

Alisha just stared at me for a minute before deciding it was in her best interest to walk away on her own.

I turned to the family and said, "I am so sorry; she pissed me off!" Kol had the biggest smile on his face.

"See, I knew we were going to cool," Candice said. "I hate that bitch, too!" Everybody started laughing.

The night went on. Charese was having a really good time with Gene. Kol and I just looked at them for a while, then laughed about what had happened.

"Do you think they have a connection like ours?" I asked Kol.

"No one else in the world could have what we have," he told me. I smiled and kissed him.

"We should get going. I don't want to look like a troll in the morning meeting your mother."

"Sam, you're beautiful, no matter what you do to yourself."

"What girl doesn't want to hear that?" We laughed and kissed each other again.

When we got in, I started packing up my things because Charese and I were leaving the next day. I was already thinking how much I was going to miss him, how I would ache since I couldn't touch him for a while.

Kol and I got in bed and he pulled me close, so I could rest my head on his chest. He began to play in my hair. I was so quiet, wondering what he was thinking.

Finally, he asked, "Why don't you just move here?"

I sat straight up. "What?"

"I love you, and the thought of you being away from me again is killing my heart. I need you with me, to see you in the morning and at night. I want you here so that I can not only send you flowers for no reason, but I want to be the one to deliver them to you. I want to be the first man you see in the morning and the last one you see at night," Kol said.

"I don't want to go on another day without you either," I told him, "but baby, I have a life in Memphis. My family is there, and I have great friends. What am I going to do about my house? And Lee would kill me!"

"Who the hell is Lee?" he asked.

"My assistant, baby. This is so big! I thought we weren't rushing things. What happened to that?"

"Do you love me, Sam? Well, do you?"

"Kol, if I didn't, would I have just showed my ass at the club like I did an hour ago? You have got to realize what you are asking me to do, what you're telling me to give up."

"For starters, I can buy your house, and we will always have somewhere to stay when we visit Memphis," Kol said.

"How much money do you make a year?"

"Well, to be honest, I work to keep myself busy, and I like telecommunications. It was my major."

"Busy? What the hell does that mean?"

"My family has a few businesses, and they are doing well," he said.

"Well?"

"Yes."

"How well?" I asked.

"Let's just say that if we just wanted to retire now, we could.

"Kol, are you serious? Why didn't you tell me about this?"

"I wanted to make sure that you were in love with me and not what I have access too. All the women in this city know about my family. I knew that if you fell in love with me, it would be with me and not the money."

"Kol, how much money are we really talking about?"

"Well," he started, "I have an accountant that I trust. I have an attorney, investment office, and I have and entire firm at my disposal. I do monitor the account balances to make sure there aren't any sudden losses. I make sure we are paying all the taxes on time."

"So, you can just buy my house and have all my stuff moved in a blink of an eye?" I asked.

"Basically, I could."

"Tell me about the family businesses."

He took a deep breath. "Candice runs three of the salons, one on the east, west, and one downtown. My other sister, Tinisha, runs two beauty supply stores, and Mike runs the five barber shops. I own quite a bit of stock in the Hyatt Corporation, where you stayed on your first trip."

"Wow. So, what's the deal with the job? Do you work there just to have something to do? When do you find time to help manage the family business?"

"I don't have to do a lot. AT&T provides all the phone and internet services in my family's businesses. I kind of lucked up on my job. I was meeting with the company rep and during the conversation, he told me about some of the benefits to working there. It just fell in my lap.

"I wanted to have some of my own money outside of the family. Don't get me wrong, my family's wealth has provided a great life for me, but I wanted to do something different in case things changed. There are a few more investments as well, but that's the bulk of it."

"Wow, I can't believe this. No wonder the girls at the club wanted your attention," I said, then something clicked in my brain. "Oh my God, you own that club, don't you?"

"Well..."

"Kol, there is so much you haven't told me, so much I don't know about you. How could you ask me to move here with so many unknowns between us?"

"Don't you love me, Sam? Isn't that enough?"

"Of course, I do, but there are so many things about you that I don't know. There are things about me that you don't know."

"Baby," he said, "we will get to know more about each other as time passes. We have a lifetime to find out new and exciting things about each other."

"This is a lot to take in. We need to have some serious conversations. I haven't been an angel ever, and there are things about me that may turn you away." I put a hand up to stop him from interrupting me with a compliment. "Also, I don't want to just leave my home, then get be sent back to it empty and alone."

"Baby, that will never happen because I love you today, tomorrow, and forever!" he reassured. "I will never turn away from you no matter what. I am not concerned with it whatever you did before me. I am only concerned with everything from September 13th and later."

"Why September 13th?"

"Because that is the first day I saw you, when I knew I would love you, and when we first spoke to each other." I looked at him and suddenly burst into tears.

"Kol, I can't believe you remembered that date!"

"Why wouldn't I?"

"I remember every moment we have shared with each other, and we will have so many dates to put together. Numbers will be our thing."

"Kol, you are wonderful in so many ways," I told him. "I know that I will love all the things I will find out about you. I already know that I love you unconditionally. You can tell me anything. I will be going home soon, and I have no idea when I can get back. In the time we have spent together, I think I know some things about you already that are key to our relationship."

"What do you mean?" he asked.

"I love the way you make love to me. It's like you have been holding on and when we are together, you just explode. You unleash so much passion, love, and things I never imagined. It's like you are holding on until you see me again.

"You are a handsome man," I continued, "and obviously, the girls at your club think so too, not to even mention Alisha! I am miles away from you, and I don't want you to feel like you are tied down with me. Kol, I love you, but I am a realist. If the women in the Chi know about you and your money, I am sure you get your fair share of Va-JJ thrown your way."

"What are you talking about, Sam?"

"Kol, I love you enough to know not to be a fool. So, what I am saying is that if you must have a chick on the side, just don't let her show her face when I am in town. She must be out of sight. No more blow ups like with Alisha."

"Have you lost your damn mind, Sam? What?"

"No, Kol, I just live in the real world. I know it's unheard of, but it's the best way for me not to get hurt. If I already know what I am walking into, it's better for me."

"Sam, you have got to be fucking kidding me? I have invited you to move here with me; you've met my entire family. I gave you a ring, a real ring, and you think I would cheat on you? I was under the impression you loved me, Sam!"

"Kol, I do love you with all I am, but –"

"But what Sam?" he cut me off. "That is so fucked up!"

"Baby," I tried to reel him in, "I don't mean to hurt you, but I just don't want to get hurt in the long run. I have got to protect myself."

"Sam, you mean everything to me," Kol said, "and I would never do that to you. You want to know the reason I am so full of passion when we are together? It's because I miss you, and when we aren't together, I want you to feel every inch of it. I want you to know how I feel when we are apart. I need you to understand the realness of our love."

"I do –"

"Sam, let me finish. I am holding onto every weak moment that I have when we are not together. I want to release all that fire, but only to you. Have you noticed, really noticed, my love patterns with you? If you did, you would know that the first day we are together, it's passionate, rough, lustful, erotic! When I see you, all I am thinking of is being inside of you. I need to feel your touch, feel your body on mine.

"Do you have any idea how hot you are? On sight, I want to take you and fuck you where you stand, have you wrapped around me. When I look into your eyes, your body calls out to me. There's electricity when we are near each other. I know you feel the pull, Sam! My dick has a mind of its own, and you are always ready for me with those wet panties.

"I want you to moan, scream, to tell me what you want me to do. I am all about pleasing you. Then, the next time we make love, it's softer. I already had a taste of you, and I want to feel every fiber of your body. I love you, and that's on everything," he said.

What a way to start making love! The moon was shining in on his skin. Kol pulled me down and pushed into my love. He sucked on the bottom of my chin as my hands glided around him. Our eyes lock, and his gaze is intoxicating. I sucked on him as my legs wrap around his back. I lifted my waist higher and came down on him. Slowly, he moved, hitting all my walls. My love tightened around him as my body convulsed and all at once, cream comes down all around him.

I fall into the silk sheets. "Sam, you're mine and I'm yours," Kol said, looking into my eyes.

"Kol, I wouldn't survive it if you hurt me," I told him.

Suddenly, he got up and went to the restroom. I heard the shower and that was my cue. I really think Kol must have been chiseled by the gods, broad shoulders, six pack, and that V-shape leading down to his glorious package, that was all mine. I got in the shower and the water ran all over us.

Kol picked up the soap and sponge and washed my body. He went from my head to my feet. It was so sexy seeing him on his knees. I thought he was about to stand up, but he washed in between my legs. When he did stand, his fingers rubbed against my stomach and breasts. It was so sensual. He went back down, going over my ass, giving me a small tap. Then, he started to kiss from the bottom up. His lips were so soft. He pushed his finger inside of me and my body begged for him.

I pushed my head back against the wall, lost as Kol dipped his tongue inside of me! He licked and sucked, getting all my juices all over him. *Lawd have mercy, I shouldn't,* I thought to myself. *I should stop him.* My knees started to buckle.

"Stop," I was finally able to breathe.

"If you really want me to…" he said, looking up, "but I don't want to." Instead of waiting for my answer, Kol pushed his tongue against my clit, making me moan.

"Kol, we're not protected like this."

"I don't care," he said. "I trust you; you're my woman. Would you ever hurt me or make me sick?"

"No, baby, I wouldn't do that to you," I answered.

"Okay then, that's solved. Relax and let me give you this pleasure. Enjoy every touch, enjoy the tip of my tongue, and the kisses from my lips. I want to taste all of you, love. You are always ready for me, baby."

Kol ran his tongue inside of me, telling me how good I tasted to him. He pulled me onto his face, not letting up at all. My body twitched, ready to release. I held his head, rubbing the back of it as he pushed in more. I could feel the build inside of me.

"Oh, baby, I'm close. I'm so close! Baby, please, or I will lose it all over your face," I moaned.

He licked deep and said, "That's what I want. Give it to me now! Come all over me, Sam!"

My own body betrayed me, and I did! Kol caught it all! I slid down the shower wall, barely breathing, and I saw his dick. *Well*, I thought, *I made it go up, so I have got to get it down.* I kissed his base, toying with his balls. I put my tongue on the center of his tip, making him grown deeply. Kol ran his hands through my wet hair. I pulled slowly and grazed my teeth on his head. When the water cooled, he carried me back to the bed and got on top of me.

"I want to make you come again," Kol said, "because I love the face you make when you come, your O face. Sam, pleasing you makes me high."

Well, he had to be high as hell because multiple orgasms were firing off. Kol had to be my weakness. He was the absolute best love I had ever had in my life.

Chapter Five

The alarm went off at 8:00 a.m. I was so tired, and I looked like it too. Kol was still holding me. My morning started with him like always, a kiss on the forehead and a good morning, Mrs. Martin.

"Good morning, my love," I said, finally sitting up. Kol burst out laughing. My hair was a mess; it was funny. It had that I had been royally fucked look. "Well, you did this, so it is your fault."

"Ok," Kol said, "I won't do it again, I promise!"

"The hell you say!" I countered. "You will do it again and again and again." We laughed, and I fell back into his arms, but I couldn't let myself get comfortable. I had to get myself together because I was meeting his mom today.

The scent of coffee traveled upstairs, and it smelled great. "Kol, I am going down for some coffee. Would you like me to bring you a cup?"

"Yes, baby."

"How do you want it?" I asked.

"Well, if you're naked, I don't care."

"Kol!" I threw a pillow at him and went down to the kitchen. Charese had brewed a fresh pot, and I knew I needed it if was going to be on point at Kol's moms.

"What the hell happened to you?" Charese asked as soon as I walked in. Then, she added, "Never mind! Damn, you look tired."

"Hell, I am," I told her, "and you don't look so rested either, Charese."

"Well, don't worry about that, Sam. Gene and I were up talking, and that's all."

"You are a grown ass woman, Charese. If you say you were talking, then you were talking."

"We were talking about you, fool."

"Honestly?"

"Yes, you and Kol to be precise."

"Why?" I asked.

"Because Gene said that Kol must really love you. He told me that Kol has always had girlfriends, but not like you. He said that women are never introduced to Kol's family like you were, that the girls usually met him wherever."

"Really?" I was astounded.

"Yeah, Gene also said he was shocked by the way Kol is with you. He said that the Alisha chick always goes back to him, but he never reacted like that before. We both think that Kol is truly in love with you."

"Well, there's something else, too. Kol wants me to move in with him. Can you believe that, me, moving to Chicago?"

"How the hell are you going to do that?"

"Charese, Kol is loaded!" I exclaimed.

"What are you talking about?"

"Kol has money, and plenty of it. He asked me to move, but I could keep my house. He would pay it off, keep the title in my name, and it could be our home when we are in Memphis visiting. Charese, I am so scared. What if I am just something to do right now?"

"Sam, it doesn't sound like those are Kol's intentions."

"I know, but what if this is all an act? What if I am the new girl for the moment? What could I offer a man that has everything and could have anyone?"

"You must have something, girl," Charese said, "because you are meeting his mom in a few hours."

"Shit, I gotta get upstairs and get dressed."

When I got up there, my things were packed, and the suitcase was on the bed for my inspection.

"Kol what have you done?" I asked.

"I have done what any good husband would do for his wife: I helped."

"Aw babe, I love you!" I gave him a hug but had to get back to business. "Okay, I have got to do something with this wig. My hair looks like a hot mess!"

"It does," he said, laughing, "and I enjoyed every moment of messing it up."

"Shut up!" I yelled, playfully. I showered and sung the entire time.

"Are you giving a free concert?" Kol asked from the door.

"No, I'm charging you with physical favors if you want a real concert," I said, and he just walked away laughing.

After an hour, finally I was ready to meet his mom, or so I thought. I was so nervous. Kol kept telling me not to worry.

"My mom will love anyone who love me," he said.

"Did she love Alisha?" I asked.

"Really, Samantha?" he said.

"Oh, did I hit a nerve?"

"Alisha has never met my mom," he said, and we ended the conversation.

We loaded the car, and I was feeling down because I knew that I would be back in Memphis soon. On top of everything, I was about to meet Kol's mom for breakfast.

"Baby, I don't want to go," I told him suddenly.

"What are you talking about, Sam?"

"I don't want to meet her yet," I answered.

"Why?"

"I am afraid this will not end well, and I just don't want to get too attached to your family."

"Sam, first, I love you, and second, don't you mean our family? Listen, trust me, please. I promise you have nothing to worry about."

"Will you just lighten up?" Charese nagged. "Don't you remember what we talked about earlier this morning?"

"Okay," I said, then took a deep breath.

We pulled up to this beautiful house with a rounded driveway. It was exquisite. The stones were beautiful, and the lawn was something straight out of *Yard Crashers*.

"This is magnificent," Charese said. "Is it only just your mom that lives here?"

"No, it's just me," Kol answered.

"Kol, this is your house?" I asked.

"Yes, I forgot something, and I need to get it before we get there." I was flabbergasted and didn't want to get out of the car. I was worried that if I went in, then I'd get this image in my head of what life with Kol would be like. The outside was bad enough. I didn't want to see what was on the inside. "Come on in," Kol encouraged. "It will just take a sec. Plus, you may want to change some stuff when you move in, so just take a look at everything now."

I balked when he said that but went inside anyway. It was like nothing I had imagined. It wasn't the typical man-cave.

Some woman had to have decorated his home. "Kol, this house is breathtaking," I sighed.

"Thanks. Candice did it," Kol said.

So, at least the woman in question was his sister. "She did a great job," I said, silently relieved.

"Yeah, she does this stuff all the time. Whenever I want a change, she comes over and just has her way with my place. It's like a guinea pig house."

"Kol, this place is straight out of my dreams." I didn't want to go any further than I already had. I was only in the front room and my feet were stuck. I couldn't move. Kol called for me to come to the back of the house.

I got my feet to finally move and listened to his voice. I walked down the hallway, spotting pictures of his family. I didn't see any pictures of his dad anywhere. I found him in the bedroom, *our* bedroom. OMG, it was huge. The bedding was chocolate brown and baby blue. There was a sitting area, two beautiful chairs and a glass table in the middle. The end of the bed had a leather trunk, along with a chaise lounge by this huge window.

"Get a good look," Kol said. "If you don't like anything, you can change whatever you want."

"No," I answered, "This place is like a dream. It feels like I'm going to wake up at any minute now."

The master bath was something of a wonder as well. The shower had two heads, an oversized tub, closed in toilets, and two sinks with a sit-down vanity. I couldn't believe that all I had to do was say yes, and everything would be mine.

It was hard to think like that. I couldn't see his home as mine, not yet. All these lavish things couldn't be my own. I heard Charese calling out to find us, and my thoughts were held at a standstill.

"Just keep walking," I told her, and she came in, grinning.

"Sam, if you don't want to stay here, then I will," Charese said.

"Are you ladies ready to go?" Kol asked. He had disappeared for a moment and was back by side. "I grabbed what I came here for."

"What did we come here for?" I asked.

"Hold out your hand," he said. I did, and he dropped a set of keys into my palm.

"What are all of these keys for?"

"These are keys to everything I have– the house, the cars, and the condo Downtown."

"Kol, I won't be here enough to use keys to all of that."

"Well, you will be soon… but no pressure."

"Right…"

We were off to his mom's place. Kol kept saying his mom would love me. It was quiet for a minute, then Charese said, "Turn that up; that's my jam!"

Hell, everything was her jam! We finally got there, and it was a beautiful home. Cars were everywhere.

"Kol, what is going on over here? Why are there so many cars?"

"It's just Sunday breakfast My mom cooks every Sunday, so my family comes over to see her, and we all get to spend time with each other."

Before we could knock on the door, it was already opening. Kol's brother, Mike, who I had met at the club when everyone was there, was at the door with a big grin. He picked me up, groaning a big "hi!" and squeezing me.

"Put me down," I laughed.

Everyone was in the kitchen which seemed like the warmest place in the world to be in. We took off our coats and joined them.

A tall, beautiful lady stood in the doorway.

"Mom," Kol exclaimed, "this is my Sam, the future Mrs. Kol Martin." I was about to tell him not to say that, but his mother just smiled. She came over and gave me the big hug.

"I am so glad to finally meet you," she said. "Kol has been talking about you, and I was wondering when I would meet you. I'm Nell."

"I'm pleased to meet you too. I've heard so much about you," I told. The nerves had left me. There was no pressure at all. I felt so warm and accepted.

"Don't believe any of it!" Ms. Nell laughed. Candice came over and snatched me away.

"Come sit by me," she whispered.

"Wait," I told her. "Ms. Nell, this is Charese, one of my best friends in the world. She's more like a sister." Charese said hi to everybody.

"Candice," Kol piped up, "I'm sorry, but Sam only sits by me. She's leaving soon, and I want to be with her every moment until she leaves." Kol was such a sweetheart. I kept waiting for the bottom to fall out, but I would enjoy every moment I could until it did. The spread of food was awesome! "Ms. Nell, you have outdone yourself," I told her. Everything looks amazing."

"Child, this is nothing. It's just a few things I put together for the kids." Ms. Nell told me. She said the grace, and it was on! I had never eaten so much food at breakfast time, but it was so good! It felt like being at my grandma's house.

When we all finished, I got up to help clear the table.

"Oh, I won't hear of it," Ms. Nell said.

"It's the least I could do," I told her, "since you've taken care of everything else."

"Okay, Kol, you better not let her go!" I loved that response!

It was Sunday, so there was football. Dallas was playing at 12:15 p.m., and our plane didn't leave until 6:00 p.m. We had plenty of time to watch the game and get to the airport on time. I wondered why we were watching the Food Network.

"Kol, can you change the TV?" I asked.

"What do you want to watch?"

"The cowboys, of course," I said.

Kol came over and gave me the biggest kiss. "I knew I would love you anyway," he said, "but to know you love football, and Dallas too, you definitely are the one."

"You are so crazy," I said. "Stop kissing me like that in front of everybody."

"Who cares? I love you and will tell the world that I am in love with you, baby. You mean everything to me." Water filled my eyes. No man had ever been this open with me before. Quite frankly, I was scared, but I wasn't going to let this one go.

Hours passed. We laughed, drank, and watched the game. Dallas won, of course. When it was time to leave, we didn't want to go, but it was time. I said my goodbyes.

"Samantha, will you be back for Christmas?" Ms. Nell asked.

"I'm not sure," I told her.

"She will be here," Kol answered, "even if I have to bring all her friends in."

"Hey, I am up for that!" Charese chimed in.

We got to the airport and unloaded all our stuff.

"Kol, I really appreciated this trip. You've been such a gentleman," Charese said "You can kidnap Sam anytime you want, just let me know when you're going to do it."

We spent the last 30 minutes laughing and talking about what fun we had, but soon, it was time to board back to Memphis.

"Don't forget to call me," Kol said.

"I won't," I told him. "I love you, Kol Martin!"

"I love you too, Mrs. Martin." He gave me a kiss to the forehead, then watched Charese and I leave. My heart broke as I left him behind.

"You will see him for Christmas!" Charese said, trying to make me feel better.

"How do you know that?" I asked.

"Because he loves you and you love him," she replied simply.

We arrived back in M-Town, and the girls were there to get us. I had missed them. The first thing they wanted to see was the ring, and it was gorgeous in the night light.

"Damn, is this real?" Lindsey asked.

"Yes, it is," I told them, "and so is this relationship. Girls, I love him with all that I am."

Once we got our bags, I called Kol, and he answered on the first ring.

"Hey, I miss you already," I said. He didn't say anything for a minute. "Are you still there?"

"No," Kol said.

"What are you talking about?"

"Turn around."

"What?"

"Turn around!"

Kol was standing behind me with his arms folded. I dropped everything and ran to him.

"What are you doing here?" I asked, jumping into his arms.

"About five minutes after you left, I just couldn't stand to be without you. I took a week off and, if it's okay, I want to stay with you?"

"I love you, fool!" Lindsey, Tammy, and Charese were came over in a hurry. "Kol, this is Lindsey and Tammy. Girls, this is Kol Martin, my man."

"Hello," Lindsey said, clearly stunned.

"Hi, how are you?" Tammy asked.

"I'm great now that I'm in Sam's arms," he replied.

"Do you have any luggage?" I asked him.

"Nope, it's just me," he answered.

"I guess we are going to have to make a stop or two," I said. "What are you going to do all day while I am at work?"

"I'm going to just enjoy waiting for you to get home."

Kol had called ahead and arranged for a car to take us home, so the girls left me in his capable hands.

For some reason, when we got to my house, I was so nervous. "Home sweet home, I said, awkwardly. Kol brought in my things and stood in the doorway.

"Where do you want these?" he asked.

"Just drop them wherever. We have more important things to do." I led Kol into the bathroom and started the shower. Love went on until the wee hours of the morning, and when the clock went off, I didn't even hear it.

"You're going to be late, baby," Kol whispered into my ear, waking me up.

"I don't care," I said, turning off the alarm and grabbing my phone. I called Lee.

"Hey, Lee," I said when he picked up. "I am a little under this morning and will be taking the day off. I think it is something I brought back from my trip."

"No worries, Sam; I will keep everything under control," Lee said.

"Okay, I appreciate it, Lee."

"Do you need me to bring you anything?"

"No, Lee, I will be just fine. I think I just need a little more bedtime." I hung up with Lee and wrapped my arms around Kol. "Okay, baby, what do you want to do today?" I asked him.

"All I want to do is you!"

"As fun as that sounds, I don't want you to get tired of it, so let's find something else to do."

"Baby, I will never get tired of you. I love you… every inch, line, and piece of you."

"Hey, we need to get you some essentials. How long are you staying again?"

"How long do you want me to stay?"

"As long as you want baby," I told him. "Let's get up and start our day. The mall is right up the street off Winchester."

We made our way to the mall to pick some things for him. We were there for so long, he started buying stuff for me.

"Kol, stop it," I told him.

"This is for you," he said. "Everything I do is for you, baby." After a while, Kol asked, "What would you be doing if I wasn't here?"

"Well, if I didn't have work. I'd be home with the fireplace burning, a glass of wine, and you on the phone."

"Okay, let's go home and do that then," he said. I called and ordered from Ruth Chris.

It was Monday night, and football was on. Kol and I snuggled in, enjoying the night.

"I'm so excited you're in town," I told Kol once we had settled into bed.

"Well, I'm excited to be here too, baby."

"What are you going to do tomorrow? You could just drop me off at work in the morning and do whatever you want to."

"No, I'll stay home and wait for you to get off."

"That doesn't sound like much fun," I told him.

"I won't have fun without you anyway," he said. "Hey, let's watch a movie. Which one?"

"I am always in the mood for *Love Jones*," I told him. "That's my favorite." He popped the movie in, but it didn't take long before I dozed off.

Chapter Six

I was up on the time the next morning. I woke up with a spark, got in the shower, and made some coffee. Kol was still sleeping, so I tried to be quiet as possible. I didn't want to wake him. I was just out the door when I head Kol clear his throat. The sound of his voice put a smile on my face.

"Are you leaving without giving me a kiss?" he asked.

"Oh, baby," I said, "I didn't want to wake you. So, you are just going to hang out all day?"

"Yep and do nothing, but rest and wait on you."

"I will see you later then, baby." I gave him the infamous forehead kiss. "I love you, and I will be home later."

I got in the office, and Lee was all over me. "How are you feeling?" he asked.

"I am great, Lee," I told him. "Just great"

"What the hell is going on with you?"

"Do you want the truth or the lie?"

"I want the truth, Ms. Thang."

"Lee, I wasn't sick yesterday. I was with Kol."

"He is the best thing to ever happen to me."

When I met him in September during the Southern Heritage Classic Weekend, I had no idea it would turn out like this. I have been in Chicago quite a bit since then, and now, he is here. He's at my house right now and will be here for about a week."

"I can't believe you have been keeping this from me all the time," Lee gushed. "This falls under the LBC (Lying Bitch Clause) too. I am so pissed at you right now."

"I'm sorry, Lee, but I am so in love, it's scary."

"Why are you scared, girl?"

"Well, it's only been two months, and he's already asked me to move to Chicago to be with him."

"What are you going to do? What about me?"

"It's too soon, Lee," I answered. "Oh, let me show you this too; look at my hand."

"Shit!" Lee exclaimed.

"Lee, calm down."

"When? How? What?"

"Will you be quiet before the whole office comes in here?"

"Damn, he is for real about you, huh?"

"It seems that way. Okay coffee, please; and let's get on with our day with no distractions."

My day was packed since I was out the office yesterday. I was making calls, monitoring and checking reports, and my God, the emails. It seemed like I had been gone for a month with all this work. Hours went by, and I decided to take a lunch. Just as I started to leave, my phone started to ring.

"Hey, baby," Kol greeted.

"I was just thinking about you," I told him.

"Really now? Well, can I come up?"

"Up where?"

"To your office, silly," he laughed.

"You're here?"

"Yes, I hope it's ok."

"Of course, it's okay. Have you gotten to the gate yet?"

"I am pulling up now."

"Tell them you are visiting me, and they will call my office," I said. I waited impatiently for a bit until there was a knock on my office door. It was Lee.

"Mr. Martin is coming up," he squealed. I did a little jump and straightened my dress.

"Be cool," I told Lee. I went to the elevators to meet Kol. He had lunch in hand and greeted me with a kiss.

"Hey, since I hadn't heard from you, I thought you might be working through lunch, so I brought you some."

"How do you know me so well already?"

"Because I pay attention to everything."

"I love you, Kol."

"I love you, Sam."

When we walked back to the office, people were trying to look so busy, but I knew what they were doing. Lee was at his desk, not even bothering to pretend. He stared at us with this kid grin he had when he was up to no good.

"Lee, this is Kol," I introduced. "Kol, this is my assistant, Lee."

"Hey, man, good to meet you," Kol said.

"Same here," Lee said. "So, Sam, are you staying for lunch now?"

"Yes, I will be in my office. If you need anything, just buzz me."

"Will do!"

We had a wonderful lunch, but finally, I had to ask Kol, "How did you get here?"

"I rented a car."

"Kol, I told you I would leave mine with you. It's no problem.".

"Oh, I don't mind. I don't want to take your car from you. I have been out and about. You know, you can get on 240 and go all over the city?"

"Way to be observant, sweetie. What are you about to do now?"

"Not much, just get into something. What time will you be home?"

"About 5:30," I answered.

"Ok, I will stay busy until then."

"You will need a key," I said. I pressed the intercom button to call Lee. "Lee, can you bring in my spare key, please?"

Lee nodded and brought the key in. I gave it to Kol, along with the alarm code.

"You did set it before you left the house, right?" I asked.

"Yes, baby, it wasn't rocket science," Kol said.

"Smart ass! I will see you later."

"Enjoy your day. I love you, Samantha."

After Kol left, Lee came in. "I am in love for you," Lee said.

"He is wonderful, Lee, in every way. I can't wait to get home, so let's kick it into high gear!"

"Yes, Mama!" he exclaimed.

5:00 p.m. came right on time.

"Lee, I am heading out, don't stay too long. I will see you bright and early in the morning."

I stopped by the liquor store to get a bottle of wine for dinner. I was planning on cooking something good, but I had no idea what! Maybe my white wine chicken. I decided to just call Kol and asked what he wanted. He told me to just come home. It sounded so good to hear him say home!

As soon as I walked in, I could smell something wonderful. So, Kol was not only good-looking and rich, but he could cook too! He met me at the door with red roses and my forehead kiss.

"Kol, what is that smell?"

"Dinner for us," he said, taking my coat and briefcase. "Now, go wash up and get comfortable. Dinner will be ready in about twenty minutes." A man had never taken care of me like this, and I was going to enjoy every second of it.

When I got to my kitchen, there was a salad, wine, lobster tails, steamed vegetables, and dessert.

"Did you cook all of this?" I asked.

"Everything, except the cheesecake. I'm not that good with deserts yet."

"Baby, this is wonderful. I thought you were going to be out enjoying yourself today."

"I did. I was getting this ready for us. Don't you know I am happy when we are happy?" he asked, pulling out my chair and kissing me on the cheek. Heart and Soul Sirius XM was playing in the background, and Kol and I were enjoying each other.

"Kol, would you like to meet my mother?" I asked him suddenly.

"Yes, I was wondering how long it would take for you to ask me."

"I haven't taken anyone by my mother's in a long time," I told him. I just don't take random guys by to see her. I will give her a call after dinner and ask when a good time would be for us to go over."

"I can't wait to meet her. What's her name?" he asked.

"It's Lue. She is great, and she is going to love you."

"How do you know?"

"Because I just do. What do you want to do now?" I asked.

"I want to do you!"

"Kol, stop playing."

"I'm not. I always want you no matter what day or hour it is. I enjoy making you feel good."

"Don't act like you don't have a good time in the process," I said.

"Oh, I do, I do indeed."

He leaned in for a kiss, but we were interrupted by the phone ringing.

"Hello? Hi, mom, what are you doing?"

"Nothing, just straightening up around the house."

"I was just talking about you."

"Oh, you were? Only good things, I hope."

"Mom, I want you to meet someone. His name is Kol Martin."

"Who is he, Samantha?"

"Mom," I said, looking deep into Kol's eyes. "He is the love of my life."

"The love of your life? Are you sure?"

Yes, Mom, he is. I have never been so in love before. He is everything and then some. I want you two to meet. He is in town this week, and I would like us to do dinner."

"How about Friday night?"

"Kol, is Friday good for you?" I asked him.

"Yes, baby. I can't wait to meet your mom," Kol said.

"Is he there now?" my mom asked.

"Yes, he came into town on Sunday," I answered

"Didn't you get back on Sunday?"

"Yes," I answered. "He told me that he missed me as soon as I left and took the next flight out. He really is great, Mom. I can't wait for the two of you to get to know each other."

"Well, I am interested to see who has my daughter so smitten," she said. "Okay then, I will let you two enjoy the rest of the evening."

"Mom, what did you call for? Did you need something?"

"No, just being nosey. I will talk to you later."

"I love you, Mom."

"I love you too, Sam."

"This is big, Kol," I said once we hung up.

"Why?" he asked.

"Because I usually don't take guys by to meet her. She is too tough on my relationships."

"I understand why, she wants the best for you. Now, she won't have to ever worry again."

"Is the Christmas invitation still good?"

"Of course, are you going to spend the holiday with me?"

"I think so. I have always been at home with my mom, though."

"You could fly out on Christmas day."

"That is going to be expensive."

"But it will be worth every penny."

"That way, I could spend Christmas Eve with my mom and the girls. We always meet at her house on Christmas Day to exchange our gifts, since it's just us."

"What about your dad? Are your parents not together?"

"No, my dad has move on with his life. I will tell Mom on Friday," I said.

"I am so excited, baby," Kol said, "to have you with me on Christmas will be wonderful! I don't know what I am going to get you."

"Kol, you have given me this beautiful ring. I don't need anything else, I am good."

"That's different. The ring was to let you know how much I love you, and Christmas is different."

"Kol, don't go overboard ok?"

"Whatever."

"Don't whatever me. What do you want?"

"I already got what I wanted: you. I love you, Sam, today, tomorrow, and forever."

"I love you too. Now, I am going to get the kitchen clean. Why don't you go find a movie on TV?"

"Sam don't worry about it. I will be here all day tomorrow, and I can take care of it," Kol said. "I want to spend this time with you."

We snuggled up on the couch. *Bad Boys II* was on. I was so comfortable with Kol, I leaned over and gave him a kiss. Let's just say I didn't leave from that spot all night. Kol and I went on like that for the rest of the week until Friday came around.

When I was in my office at work, I received a bouquet from Kol, reminding me of the meet and greet with mom that day. He was clearly excited. When I got off, I headed straight home. Kol was ready and waiting on me. That night, we were going to the Butcher Shop, my mom's favorite. When we left to pick her up, Kol was nervous. I told him it would be fine. We got there, and I let us in with my key.

"Mom, we're here," I announced loudly. "Where are you?"

"The bedroom," my mom yelled.

"Kol, just have a seat on the couch," I told him.

I went to her room, and she looked great! I hated going out with her sometimes because she was truly the pretty one. "Mom, you look amazing," I told her.

"Where is he?" she asked.

"Sitting in the front. He is so worried, but I told him to just stay cool," I said, and she just laughed.

"Well, lead the way to your man," she said. When we got to the living room, Kol stood with a smile.

"Kol, this is my mom, Lue, and Mom, this is Kol," I said.

"I am pleased to meet you," my mom said.

"The pleasure's all mine, Lue. I see where your beautiful daughter gets her good looks."

"Well, Sam, I see why you like him. He is a charmer," my mom said.

"Let's go," I said.

When we arrived at the restaurant, I couldn't believe Kol sat by her, right in the middle of us. They talked like old friends, like he was no stranger. I was so excited and happy because they were getting along great.

"I have something to ask you," Kol said to my mom.

"Okay, what is it?" she asked.

"Well, I want Sam to spend Christmas with me. She told me about your celebration on Christmas Eve. So, I wanted to know if I can steal her away from you on Christmas Day, please? She would be taking late flight, but not too late. I want her to get in before it's dark, but also give you time to spend together. I wanted to make sure it was ok with you before we made any major plans."

"This is a surprise, Sam. Where did you find him?"

"Mom!"

"Any man that appreciates the relationship you have with your mother is alright with me."

"Of course, I do," Kol said. "You're the woman that raised her."

"Well, Kol, while I appreciate you asking and thank you for being a man, Sam is a grown woman. However, this type of chivalry isn't seen too often these days," Mom answered.

"Well, I appreciate you feel that way," he told her.

"Besides," my mom added, "Sam and I always spend time together. A Christmas away will be good for her."

"You two realize I am sitting right here," I interjected.

"Thank you so much, Ms. –" Kol started.

"No, Kol, it's Lue for now," my mom said.

"I want to thank you, Lue," Kol continued, "and I want you to know that I love Samantha with all I am. I want to spend today, tomorrow, and forever letting her know that.

"Thanks, baby, I love you, too, but stop it with the Samantha," I said. "It's Sam! Kol, you have never said that in front of anyone before. Mom, see? He is the one!"

Dinner was great. When we left, the I-40 was crowded that night, but who cared? I was with Kol, and that was all that mattered. We dropped off my mom and got home. Kol opened the door for me, and I was in my own dream.

We started a conversation about Christmas. The flight would be high, especially since we were getting it last minute.

"No worries, Sam," Kol told me. "I want you there and will pay any price."

That night, Kol decided he didn't want to leave me tomorrow and extended his trip.

I rolled over about 4:00 a.m. and looked at Kol sleeping beside me. That man was beautiful. As though he felt my eyes on him, suddenly, he put his arms around me. I just couldn't help myself.

"Kol, let me have my way with you," I told him. I knew I was going to be tired at work later that morning. It was Saturday, but I had to go in for a few hours on because I left work early all week. When it was time to get up, I just laid there. I was tired as hell.

"I want to stay in bed with you," I groaned.

"Then, why won't you?" Kol asked.

"I have to go, Kol."

"You don't have to go, Sam. You just want to."

"I can't just not go. Are you being crazy?"

"If you wanted to," Kol said, "you could quit and run away with me now. We can have everything set up for Christmas and your family can come to Chicago for the holidays."

"Kol, I just can't do that."

"Why not?" he asked.

Chapter Seven

"Wow, that was an inconsiderate thing to say, Kol," I said. "You aren't giving up anything, but I am. I must give up my family, friends, and a career that I worked damn hard to build. You already have everything with you."

"Baby, I am sorry," Kol said immediately. "That was so insensitive of me. I just want you to be with me so badly."

"I get it, but remember: baby steps, okay?"

"Okay," he agreed. "Just don't be made at me.".

I got out of the bed, thinking about what he said, and the truth was I wish I could. I wished I could just up and go without a care in the world. *What about my mom? What about my girls? What about me?* Was that what I wanted, or was I just having a good time right now?

I quickly got myself ready for work and was just about to leave. Kol grabbed my hand. "Sam, please forgive me," he said.

"For what?" I asked him, distracted by my thoughts.

"I was out of line when I said that stuff earlier. I am so sorry, baby."

"Kol, it's ok. I get it; I do."

"Sam, I made you some breakfast."

"When did you do that?" I asked.

"Well, I wanted to make up. I should have never said those things."

"I am fine, Kol. Look, I am going to be late. I'll call you later," I said, before rushing out.

Lee met me in my office. "Your new boyfriend must have pull somewhere," he said, "because you already have flowers waiting this morning."

"Are you serious?" I asked, trying to hold in the smile forming on my face.

"Did yall have a little spat this morning?" he asked.

"No, Lee, things are great. I may even be leaving by Christmas."

"What are you talking about?"

"I know this is a lot to handle this early, but I haven't had coffee."

"Yeah, and we have so much to get done. Let me get you a cup, and we'll talk about it later."

"Thanks, Lee," I said as he disappeared out of my office.

Even though I had work to do, I am ending up calling the girls. As soon as they answered the phone, I confessed, "Girls, I'm really considering moving to Chicago." They all wanted to meet for lunch, so we did.

"Are you going to do it?" Lindsey asked.

"I don't know, but guess what? Lue loves him," I said.

"You're lying," Charese said.

"Nope," I replied, "We had dinner last night. She is so cool about this, and I am scared to tell you the truth. My mom doesn't like anybody."

"Well, she can see how happy you are with him," Lindsey said. "I think we all see it, Sam."

"Tammy, what do you think?" I asked. She was the only one who hadn't weighed in on it today.

"I don't know, Sam. I don't know him well enough to judge him, but I do know you, and I haven't seen you this happy ever," Tammy said. "Take this happiness and have it for as long as you can, Sam. Life is short, and you only get one-real chance at the love of a lifetime. I think Kol is it for you. I say go and be happy."

"Thanks, Tammy," I told her. "I love you. I love you all, but I must think about it just a little more. Look, girls, I have got to get back. I will get with you all later."

Lunch was great. I listened to what the girls had to say, *but what was my heart saying?* I thought. Kol was the one I had been waiting for all my life, but this was moving so fast. I wanted to be sure that he was what I need and not just someone I was having great sex with. I would give it until the end of the year. I'd known him since September, but it seemed like forever in a good way.

When I got home, Kol was gone. I had no idea where he was or what he was doing. I did the usual: got comfortable and started on some dinner. I wanted pork chops, grilled asparagus, and maybe some corn. I cranked up the music and got in the kitchen.

About an hour later, Kol came in, all smiles.

"Hey, babe, hey. Did you have a good day at work?" he asked, giving me a kiss on the cheek.

"It was fine," I answered. "What about you?"

"You know," he said, "I had no idea Memphis was so small." I made a face. "I know," he laughed, "but it's cute… just like you. You cooked?"

"Yes, why?"

"I was going to take you out for dinner," said Kol, looking a little disappointed.

"Kol, we ate out last night," I said.

"I know, but I want to spoil you while I'm here. That way, you will miss me even more when I'm gone."

"Shut up and get washed up. Don't remind me you're leaving me," I said.

Another week had winded down, and it was time for him to leave. Our last night together was coming to a close, and we didn't want to do anything, no TV, radio, or movies.

I just wanted to ball up and cry. He wanted to get out, but I just wanted to be with him, and him only. "Kol, I don't want you to go! I know it's selfish of me, but I can't stand the thought of you leaving in the morning," I said.

"Then, I will stay longer," he said.

"Kol, you can do that?"

"I can, and I will for you," he said. When he said that, it made me think that this man was willing to do everything for me. He'd change his whole lifestyle to make me happy.

"Kol," I said, "I want to do it."

"That was easy. I thought I was going to have to put on a big show for the last night of love making," Kol said.

"Not that you fool. I mean, us. I want to be with you for as long as you'll have me."

"Babe, are you for real?"

81

"Yes, this feeling that I have right now is almost unbelievable," I said. "You know, I have been up a lot while you were sleeping, and I would just look at your face and love you so much. Just waking up next to you, that smile of yours, and having you here when I get home, it has been something I never dreamed of.

"Kol, the way I love you is pure. It's like being in a new world, and we are the only two there. I love you so much that I can feel you touch me when we are apart. My thoughts of you are almost like magic. I smile whenever I think of you, and it gets wider and wider with every thought. I realized that happiness is something that I want forever, and I want forever with you, Kol. I love you, and I want to move to Chicago for Christmas."

"Sam, are you sure, really sure?"

"Yes, baby, I am!" I exclaimed. Kol charged me and lifted me in his arms. "Kol, you are going to squeeze me to death."

"Baby, I am so happy. I love you Sam! I can't wait to tell my family," Kol said.

"Wait, Kol, I have to put in for a transfer," I said. "I won't just quit my job. I love it too much. I have so many things to do. I have got to tell my mom and the girls too. And what about Lee? He is going to be so mad. He's been my assistant for quite some time now."

"Baby, no worries. The transfer won't be a problem at all. Which location do you want to go to?" Kol asked.

"What do you mean? Please tell me you don't have…"

"Well, I do have a seat at FedEx, so I am pretty sure it won't be a problem."

"Damn, you are serious!" I exclaimed.

"Baby just let me know, and I will start making calls ASAP!

"Kol, just because you have a seat and investments doesn't give you the right to just hand something to me."

"But Sam, I am serious about us. I love you, and I will move heaven and earth for you," he said.

I was so excited to think that Kol and I would be having our first Christmas together. We began to make love, and it seemed to just keep getting better and better and better. That very night, the last night we had before he is going home, he made me cry tears of joy.

It was morning, and I didn't want to let him go. Kol was leaving and I was beyond sad.

We had breakfast and took back the rental. It was quiet between us. We just held hands and shared long stares. I didn't want to talk. We finally started to get things in order and talked a little about the move. We stopped by my mom's, so Kol could say goodbye.

Soon, it was time, and we kissed as long as we could. "Kol," I said. "While you're away, I'll start looking for a transfer location. Would you please call me when you get home?"

"I will call you when I land and talk to you on the way to our home," he replied.

"I love you, baby."

"I love you too, Sam."

I was so unhappy when Kol left. It felt like a piece of me was missing. I tried to stay busy while I waited on him to call, but I couldn't. I went home and just sat down. I waited and waited. I was just starting to get worried when he finally called.

I logged onto the company website, and there were positions available for the Chicago location. I planned to get with my supervisor's tomorrow instead of just posting for the job because I felt like I needed to keep my superiors in the loop. About 3 hours passed before Kol called again.

"What the hell have you been doing?" I asked. "Did you fall asleep or something?"

"No, I just can't wait for you to get here," he said.

"Kol, what have you been doing?"

"I have been on the phone with a few people discussing business."

"You just got back and it's Sunday. Tell me the truth now."

"Okay, the truth is that I have made a few calls about the positions here in your department. When you get ready, just send me your resume, and someone will call you to let you know when you can start."

"Kol," I said, exasperated, "I don't want to be handed a job because of you. I want to earn it. You are going about this all wrong. I want to be selected for what I do with my skills and knowledge because I do my job well."

"Sam, I just wanted you here so badly, and when you agreed to come, I wanted to do everything in my power to make it happen."

"Kol, I understand your point of view, but is this how my life is going to be now? Will I just have to live in your shadow and have things handed to me? I won't live like that. I am worth every penny that I demand and then some. I will not be given anything. I wasn't raised that way and I refuse to start doing that now."

"Sam, please don't be made with me. I love you, and I do get it."

"I am really upset right now," I told Kol. "Maybe you should just get settled in since you were so busy making calls, and we will talk in the morning."

"In the morning? We never go to be without talking," he said.

"I realize that," I replied. "Look, I just need to sort some things out right now, and I am not in the right frame of mind to be the Sam you love. If you wanted a woman who depended on you for everything, I am not what you want."

"That's not what I want, Sam," Kol tried to say, but I was too fired up.

"I am not the woman that needs you to define me. I already know who I am. I love you with all I am, but I won't love me any less trying to love you, Kol. Look, I better go, and I will call you in the morning."

"Sam, I love you," Kol said. "I know, and I love you too."

"Good night, Kol," I said before hanging up the phone.

Chapter Eight

What am I going to do? I thought. I couldn't live like this! This changes everything. We hadn't talked about all the financials! How could I just walk into a move that big so blindly? *Damn, I let his dick control the shit out of me.* I knew I loved him and our love was real, but I just wanted to be with him so much. The man was intoxicating. Was giving up my freedom the price for the man I loved?

I got together a list of questions. Kol and I needed to make sure we were on the same page before we go any further. I was upset, but did I have a right to be? Kol was just trying to help.

It was morning, and Kol hadn't called me. I guessed he is giving me the time I needed. Maybe he wanted a trophy girl. Maybe he had some things to think about too now. He probably spent the morning reevaluating our relationship. *Good God, I hope he didn't want to end things!*

I decided that I had better give Kol a call to clarify before my mind drove me insane. I listened to the phone *ring, ring, ring* before, *please leave your message for Kol Martin.*

What the hell? Kol always answered my call. He must have really been upset, but he should have understood how I felt, too. I decided to take a shower, and hopefully, that would help me relax. I could try him again when I get out.

I got in the shower and my mind was racing, trying to figure out what Kol was thinking. I heard the sound of my alarm being deactivated. Panic shook through me, but I reasoned that it had to be one of the girls or moms. *Why, though?* They don't usually just pop up. *What's happened?*

"Sam?" I heard a voice call.

"Kol?" I gasped.

"Where are you?" he yelled.

"I'm in the shower," I replied. "What are you doing back here?"

"I didn't mean to hurt you like that," he said through the door. "You were right; I was only thinking of myself and not thinking of us. Please say you will forgive me?" he asked.

"Kol, I can't believe you flew back. What were you thinking?" I got out of the shower and wrapped a towel around myself.

"I was thinking that you didn't want us anymore, and I came to change your mind. Sam, I was out of line again. I should have waited on you and waited to see how you wanted to take care of things," he said. "This is your life too, and I should respect that!"

"Kol, all was forgiven the second you came home. You amaze me with the stuff you do. You are crazy as hell, but if you would do this for me, you must be in love with me," I said.

"Did you ever doubt it?"

"Well, for a minute I wondered what I was to you. Was I just the girl you picked up from down South?"

"Sam, no matter how I behave, or what I do, I will love you until the day I can't breathe anymore. Girl, you give me something I have never had in a woman, pure peace," said Kol. "I wake up and thank God for you and us every day! I am so in love with you woman that I would –"

"Baby, stop. I'm the sorry one. I think we need to talk about how we are going to do this. Wait, don't you have work in the morning?"

"I don't have to be in the office to work, remember? I can work from anywhere, and here is where I need to be."

"Kol, you would do that for me?"

"No, I would do it for us," Kol said. My towel hit the floor as I wrapped my arms around his neck. I kissed him and wanted Kol so badly. My body started to tingle. I shivered and my skin prickled.

I lead Kol into my bedroom and pushed him down on the bed. I lit every candle in my room and was on top of him in no time. I took off his shirt, and our skin felt like it was fused together! My tongue was tingling from the taste of him.

I pulled his belt off, and everything it was holding up. Kol pulled me close to him, and I couldn't move.

"Sam, l love you," he whispered in my ear. "Forever is what I want with you. I can't explain how much I love you, but if you let me, I can show you right now."

"I want this forever too," I told him. I leaned down and kissed his chest with small kisses. He held my hands, but I had to get them free to do what I wanted. I grabbed his dick and played with it gently. He liked it from the rumble I heard from him. I slowly kissed the tip, then down the side, the bottom of his balls.

As I licked my way back up, I could feel his dick throbbing. I put my mouth over the head with my tongue, swirling around it. I opened my mouth wide and flattening my tongue, so I could go down to the bottom, controlling my breathing. With every deep breath, I went deeper.

He pulled my waist onto his chest, and I never stopped pleasing him. He pulled my butt closer to his face, closer and closer until his lips were kissing my bottom lips. We were both locked in a position where we could both enjoy. The more he got me off, the more I moaned and squirmed, but he wouldn't let me go. I had come up for air, and when I did, he pushed me back into the headboard, turned me over, and began again.

He only broke away to say, "Fuck my face, ride it hard so I can have all your delicious cream!"

I motioned for him to turn over on his side, so he could slide in from the back. As we got closer, the anticipation of having him inside me made my temperature rise. He was finally inside me. His arm held my breasts, pulling from one nipple to the other nipple.

His other hand held onto my thighs tightly and slid down between my legs! My body was no longer mine. It was Kol's now, and it obeyed him!

"Come for me, baby," he said. "Come hard for daddy. Give it to me now! I won't ask you again!" I pushed to him faster, harder I tried to stop because I wanted this all night, but my body betrayed me.

There was an explosion everywhere! Kol was so deep inside me, I was shaking! It was a whole new spill! Kol was official; he was certified; he was perfect, and now, the only man to find my G-Spot! Kol rose, rolled me over, pushed my legs open, and again, hit the bottom of my love!

My body screamed for more and more of his love, and he gave it to me. Kol was loving on me like it as the last time. He wrapped one of my legs around his shoulder, so he could be deeper inside of me. He was so gentle, but he gave me what I needed. I lost myself while he was inside me!

As his love let go, he kissed me, and I felt his warmth spilling inside me. He pulled the covers over our bodies as he touched my face. "I will never make you unhappy again," Kol said.

"Well, if you do, I will take this as an apology anytime," I replied. We laughed and laid there, finally breathing easy.

When he started to get up, I touched his arm. "Where are you going?" I asked.

"Nowhere. I will be right back." He came back with drinks and wanted to know if I wanted him to run a bath.

"Lawd, have mercy! You can't be real. Baby, all I want is for you to come back to bed," I said. We made love again and I slept until the sun came up.

I hated my alarm clock. I could hear Kol in the kitchen and went to follow all the noise.

"Baby, what in the world are you doing?" I asked.

"Making omelets for you."

"That sounds good. Let me go take a quick shower. I'll be right back." In the shower, I could feel him from the night before.

We had breakfast and laughed the entire time, but I wanted to make sure I was clear before I left for work.

"Kol, when I get home, we have to talk about our future," I said before leaving.

The day couldn't go by fast enough. I finally got home, and Kol was waiting for me. Kol had ordered dinner and picked it up, so we could concentrate on us.

"How was your day?" he asked.

"It was okay. I kept thinking about us," I admitted, sitting beside him.

"Me too," he replied. "We have plenty of time to discuss everything."

"So," I said, "where do we start?"

"Well, I think I should take care of the bills. I don't think you should be responsible for anything major."

"What about my own bills, like credit card debt or this furniture I'm still paying on?" I asked.

"Sam, when I got you, I got your debt. I can take care of that, too. If you want to continue to take care of it, then you can if you want. In fact, you can pick any household bill to handle, and you can do all the shopping for anything we need at home."

I was all smiles because he wanted me to do what I wanted to do. "Kol, I'm happy you're letting me take on some of the financial burden. Everything sounds fine with me, babe."

"Hey, if we are going to be together, then we are together," he replied.

"Would you like to open a new account for bills only?" I asked. "That way, we can just move money into it as needed. We could also have a portion of our payrolls go in there too.

Whatever needs to be paid, we will just pay it from that account."

"Okay, I like that idea. Let's also agree that we will never spend a large amount of money without the other one's knowledge," Kol added.

"That sounds fair to me," I said.

"Well, that was easy, baby. When are you leaving for Chicago?"

"Fool, I have to put my house on the market and get a job first."

"We can keep the house, remember? The job will be there; you are talented, smart, and your beauty doesn't hurt. Someone will call."

and the next morning, I dropped Kol off at the airport.

"I can't wait until you are on this flight with me," he said.

"I love you," I said.

"I love you too."

When I got in to work, Lee reminded me of the meeting I was to have with my bosses was at 10:00 a.m. I killed the hour and a half by staring at the clock, feeling anxious about how they would take the news. When he time came around, I entered the room and blurted out that I was planning to move.

"However, I do want to stay with the company," I explained. "It has nothing to do with anyone here. I think you guys are amazing and I love my team. It's just that I am getting married soon and want to be closer to my soon to be husband."

My supervisor, Aaron, was very supportive and shook my hand. The other supervisor, Karen, gave me a hug and asked to see my rind.

"If you need anything," Karen said. "A recommendation, a connection, you name it, give me a call."

I went back to my office feeling elated and started reviewing open positions on the computer. I found one and sent in my resume. I thought that I wouldn't hear anything for maybe a week, but a few hours later my phone rang.

Chapter Nine

The phone interview went well. I had a pleasant conversation with a Mr. Parker at the department in Chicago. The whole thing lasted about twenty minutes or so, and I was promised to have an answer very soon.

"Hey, how's your day going?" Kol asked when he called around lunch.

"Great, but I am missing you something awful," I replied.

"Same, same."

December came quickly. Mr. Parker offered me a great position with a salary I couldn't turn down. It was almost time for Christmas. Kol and I had planned so many things, from decorations to rearranging the house. We talked every day and every night. He wanted to come down every weekend, but I told him if I didn't, he would miss me more.

I hated being away from him. The month was passing by so fast, and it was finally time to fly out. I had dinner with my mom and the girls. We were all crowded up in Mom's den, laughing and opening gifts. We had drinks and cried about how far away we would be from each other.

"Come on, it's just 8 hours away by car and an hour flight," I said. "We will be together all the time."

"Yes," Charese said, "and the last time I checked, everyone's phone, email address, and social media accounts were still working, so you have no excuse not to contact us."

"Yeah," Lindsey chimed in, "I don't care how swept away in love you are, you need to let us know how you are on the daily."

"I will, girls," I said and turned to my mom. "Mom, I love you so much. Thank you for everything you've done to raise me to this point in my life," I told her. Her eyes became misty and she hugged me, like it was the last time. When the night came to an end, the girls dropped Charese and I off at my house. They each promised to keep an eye on my home while I was away.

Charese stayed over that night to drop me off at the airport in the morning. I only had three bags packed. Kol and I would come back to pick up the rest of my things later. As I got ready for bed, I started to feel sick. I didn't know what was going on. I felt a little funny earlier in the week.

I called Kol. "Babe, I'm sick," I told him. "I'm not sure if I can make the flight tomorrow."

"Look, don't worry. Everything will be fine, just get some rest and let me know how you feel after," said Kol.

Charese got me some ginger ale, and I started to feel a little better. "Is it time for your cycle?" she asked. I thought about it, and it was late, but that was normal for me.

"My cycle jumps around like Michael Jordan," I said, she made a crazy face.

"Maybe you are," she said.

"No, I couldn't be. It's not the right time or anything."

"Whatever. I am going to Walgreens to get a test, and if Mrs. Linda isn't there, I will be right back.

She came right back. "Mrs. Linda wasn't there huh?" I asked.

"Nope. Now, go pee on the stick!"

We waited and in about 10 minutes, two pink lines went across the tube.

"You are shitting me," Charese exclaimed.

"What Charese, what?" I asked.

"You're pregnant!"

"No, I can't be."

"Too late, Sam. Oh my God, when are you going to tell Kol?"

"I don't know," I screamed. "We haven't even talked about kids. I don't even know if he wants kids. What am I going to do?"

"Well, at least you don't have to give him a gift. You were so worried. Now, you got something... someone!"

"Charese this isn't funny, stop playing."

"I'm not, Sam. He is going to be thrilled."

I couldn't sleep, and before I knew it, morning had creeped upon me.

"Let's get to the airport now.," I told Charese, who was dragging her feet. "I am so nervous."

"Your phone is ringing," Charese said, bringing it to me. "It's Kol."

"Hey, how are you? Are you ready to go?" he asked.

"Charese is here getting ready to drop me off now," I replied.

"Good, I can't wait to wake up in your arms tomorrow."

"Yeah, me too."

"Hey, are you feeling alright? Last night, you told me you weren't feeling too well," Kol answered.

"Yeah, I'm just being careful. I have been feeling sick the last couple of days. It must be me being love sick. I can't wait to see you."

"Me too, I love you."

We hung up and I le tout a loud scream.

"What is wrong with you?" Charese asked, looking at me like I had three heads.

"How am I going to tell him, Charese?"

"Just do it! He loves you, and I am sure he will love this baby, too."

"Whatever. Let's go. My flight's leaving in two hours." When we got to the airport, the girls were waiting.

"You didn't think we would let you let you go without saying goodbye, did you?" Lindsey said, giving me a big hug.

"I will miss you so much!" I said, holding onto her tightly.

"Ditto kid!"

"Flight 210 to Chicago is at gate A3," said a voice over the intercom.

"I will call you guys when I land," I said, hugging each of them.

"Okay, Sam, and don't forget to tell us what Kol said about the baby!" Charese blurted.

"Baby?" Lindsey and Tammy said in unison.

"What the hell are you talking about, Charese?" Lindsey asked.

"Shit," Tammy said, "I knew someone was pregnant because I have felt weird all week."

"Look, it's nothing to get excited about," I said. "It was just a pee on a stick. When I get to my new OB/GYN, I will let you know. Now, I have got to go. I love y'all!" I left before they could ask any more questions. Alone now, my mind was going in so many different directions. I had to face the music!

"Baby, you're here," I said, jumping into Kol's arms.

"I am so happy to see you," he said, holding me tight.

"Kol are you ok?"

"I just feel a little queasy, but I am fine now that you are here. Let's get your bags. I'm so happy. It's almost Christmas and I already got my wish, you! Let's get out of here."

When we got home, I really just wanted to lay down.

"Can I have Candice's number?" I asked.

"Why? Is there anything wrong?" Kol asked, concerned.

"No, baby, I just need to find new doctors. Since I'm off until the first of the year, I figured I will get all my check-ups done."

"Oh, okay. Now, that your bags are down, you want to go out for dinner?"

I just wanted a shower and to hit those sheets. "Baby, can we just curl up tonight?" I asked. "I am not feeling so hot."

"Are you okay, Sam?"

"Yes, I feel fine," I lied.

"I guess we should stay in. I feel kind of woozy myself," he said.

"Do we need to go to the hospital?" I asked, feeling his head. "Oh, my God, you are sick!"

"Baby, I am okay. I am going to the doctor the day after tomorrow. I have been sick like this for about a week now. I thought it was just a virus or something, but I can't shake it."

Wait until he finds out he can't shake me for at least 18 years, I thought. "Baby, I'm sure you will be fine. I bet it's nothing."

"No, Sam, something is wrong with me. I am never sick. I went by my mom's yesterday and she said the strangest thing to me."

"What did she say?"

"She told me 'it's a wonderful surprise and just be happy.' I had no idea what she was talking about, but since I didn't feel good, I just said ok."

Well, if that wasn't the push I needed. "Kol, I have something to tell you," I said.

"What is it?" he asked, taking a seat on the couch.

"I don't know how I am going to do this," I mumbled, but he heard.

"Do what? Are you thinking of going back to Memphis?"

"No, nothing like that," I said, almost laughing. "I just don't know how I can say this. I'm not even certain. It could be something totally different, but I do think we need to talk about it."

"What is it?" he pressed.

"It's just so rough even thinking about saying it out loud."

"Sam, nothing could be that bad. You are my angel. Baby, you can tell me anything and you know it."

"I think I might be pregnant."

"What? Pregnant? are you sure?"

"No, I'm not, and I knew you would be upset. I shouldn't have told you. I'm so sorry, Kol," I said, and for some reason, I started crying. Kol gathered me into his arms. "It was just a test from the store, and that's why I wanted to get to Candice's doctor ASAP."

"You actually think I am upset?" he asked. "Sam, I couldn't be happier. I'm just shocked, sweetheart. I can't believe I am going to be a daddy. Sam, let's get married now!"

"Now? Kol, I may or may not be pregnant. I haven't gone to the doctor to confirm it yet. I must be sure, and if I am, who's to say we should get married now?"

"Baby, I know, but I'm so excited. I'm so ready for us to start our lives together."

"This is a lot to take in right now. Can we just get through the night first?"

"Okay baby, I am just so excited. Do you want a pillow and blanket or something? Whatever you want I will get it. I hope it's a girl – no, a boy, no I just want a healthy baby."

"Stop it," I groaned.

"I'm going to be a dad. I can't wait. I love you, Sam! Have you told anyone yet?"

"Only the girls. Charese was there when I took the test, and she slipped at the airport to everyone else."

"I am going to call Candice and Mike right now."

"Kol, wait, I want to be sure before anyone else finds out," I said.

"That's not fair, you got to tell someone."

"I know, but that's —" He made a face. "Okay, but just the two of them. I don't want to jinx it."

"Babe, they are going to be so excited, almost as happy as I was"

"Honestly, I'm surprised you don't already have kid, Kol. You're the prime target for most women."

"Sam, I told you I was waiting for the right one. I was waiting on you. I knew you would show up in my life, but I didn't know when. I would wait until the end of time for you and our family. I knew when I saw you that day I would have a life with you, and I wasn't going to take no for an answer. Thank God for the Southern Heritage Classic! Baby, you make me so happy."

"Will you put your arms around me, Kol?"

The next morning, I got just what I wanted Christmas… morning sickness.

"Are you ok, baby?" Kol asked.

"Fine, just give me a few minutes," I said into the toilet. "This shit has got to stop. I can't take this another 9, 8, or however many months it is."

"I'm sure it'll get better with time. I don't think morning sickness lasts the whole pregnancy." I got up to brush my teeth again and grimaced at myself in the mirror. "My love, you look beautiful," Kol said, as if on cue. "Merry Christmas, Sam."

"Merry Christmas to you too. Would you like some coffee, honey?"

"No, baby, you just rest."

"Kol, I am not helpless, just barely pregnant, if I am."

"Don't say that, you are pregnant, and I am happy about this."

"Calm down, we will find out next week for sure. I am so nervous about this new life we will have. Shit!"

"What is it?"

"What if I am pregnant? What about the new job?"

"I guess you're not working."

"You're joking."

"Maybe start your own business," Kol suggested. "You could always stay home until you find something you want to do."

"Are you serious? I could just stay home until I am ready to work?" I asked him.

"Baby, you can, I already told you that. I take care of everything now anyway, and I will continue to do that, so what's a few more things to take on? Are you sure you want to start out like this? Three months together, and I am already pregnant," I said.

"So, what? We're going to welcome this baby into this world," Kol said.

"I bet your family is going to think I am a gold digger now. This is too much to process, too soon. We won't have any alone time to just enjoy each other if we do this."

"Don't worry about it. Don't worry about anything. Everything will work out for the better."

"Kol, I have a mortgage just in case you have forgotten!"

"No, I haven't forgotten. I can pay it off now if you want. Monday perhaps?"

"But it's my house, Kol," I said.

"No, baby, it's our house."

"Fine," I gave in. "Hey, if you are planning on spoiling me, then, go for it!" He laughed and gave me a kiss. "I have got to call my mom," I told him. "This is the first year we haven't been together on Christmas."

"I am grateful that your mom was okay with you coming."

"Let me give her a call. I need her to know how much I appreciate her." When my mom picked up, a wide grin spread across my face. "Hi, Mom. Merry Christmas. Kol wants to talk to you."

I handed the phone over. "Merry Christmas, Lue."

"Hey, Kol, Merry Christmas to you too, son."

"I just wanted to call you and say thanks for allowing me to have Sam this Christmas, I really appreciate you!"

"Kol, you know all I want is for Sam to be happy, and from the looks of it, you are the one that is responsible for that. I am proud to call you, son!"

"Thank you. Alright, here's Sam again."

"Hi mom!" I greeted her again. "I miss you so much, and I hate that I am not there with you."

"Nonsense, Sam, you are exactly where you need to be. I hope you're enjoying every moment of this. Life is short!"

"Okay Mom, I love you, and I will call you later ok?"

"Ok, baby, have a good time."

"Ah, I miss her so much," I groaned once the line went dead.

"I know, baby, but we can go visit her for New Year's if you want?"

"That would be wonderful!"

"Then it's set. We will book the flights tomorrow. Let's get ready to hit my mom's house. This is going to be something!"

"What do you mean something?" I asked.

"Well, it gets crazy on Christmas at my mom's since all the kids and grandkids will be there. It can be a bit much to take in, but you will be fine."

"I hope so. Let's get started!"

Chapter Ten

"Kol, it won't be that crazy, will it?" I asked him on the way to his mom's.

"Yes, it will!" he said.

Candy was the first one out the door when we arrived.

"Sam, hey girl! You look too cute," she said, giving me a hug. "Hey Kol." She play-punched her brother.

"What up, Candy?" I said.

"Girl, I can't wait until you start showing!"

"Candice, we haven't confirmed anything yet. We're going to the doctor's this week, so don't say a word."

"Wait, what? I thought this was good news for everybody," she said with a stunned look on her face.

"Candice, you didn't?" I gasped.

"Sorry, I was so excited when Kol called. I was here at Mom's already, so it just kind of came out."

"Kol!" I hissed.

"Sam," he said, "it will be ok. Candice, you owe us one."

"I know, and I will make it up to you, I promise."

"Let's get this over with," I grumbled.

"Hey mom," said Kol. I tried to hide behind him. "How are you?"

"Sam, baby," his mom said, "come on in! I am so glad you three are here."

"Hi, Nell," I said, unsure of how she'd receive me. She embraced me in a strong hug.

"I am so proud of you and Kol," she said with tears in her eyes.

"Mom, we just got here," Kol said.

In an instant, the whole family was falling over me. I started to feel sick. There were too many people, all pulling me in for hugs and talking all at once. It was hot and the longer I stood there, the more I felt like I needed to hurl.

"Kol, I need to go outside for a second," I whispered.

"Baby are you ok?"

"I feel queasy. It's a little too hot."

"Let's go, baby. I don't want you feeling uncomfortable."

"Is everything ok?" Nell asked.

"Yeah, we will be right back," he said.

As soon as I got out the door, I threw up. It was nasty. "Do you need anything?" Kol asked, rubbing my back.

"Kol, could you get me a cool towel and maybe a Sprite. Your mom is going to be so mad at me."

"I don't think she will care at all. She is just happy we are here and expecting to bring another generation of Martins into this world. Are you ok? Do you want to stay out here or go back inside?"

"Inside; it's cold. I just had a moment I guess."

"Is everything all, right?" Nell asked when we returned.

"Yeah, we are fine," Kol answered. "She just got hot for a second."

It was a long day. There was dinner, gifts, and being surrounded by the family. I had so much fun, and it seemed I blended right in. After having a wonderful time with the family, it was time for Kol and I to go home.

"Mom, thanks for everything," he told her on the way out. She was smiling extra hard at Kol.

"Baby, didn't I tell you it would be a great surprise?"

"Yeah, but Mom, how could you have known?" he asked.

"I am a mother, and your mother. I know my children and their children before they are even born. I knew every single time one of your sisters was expecting before they did. It's a gift. I love you, son. You two have a good night. Be safe getting home."

I was so tired. When we got home, all I wanted was to go to bed.

"Hey, let me run you a bath," Kol offered.

"That sounds wonderful." When he called me in after a bit, I was floored. "Kol! Candles, music, and snacks? If I didn't know any better, I would think you were trying to seduce me."

"Well, is it working?"

I settled into the bath tub. "Why don't you come join me and we will see?"

"Let me wash your back for you," he said. The water he poured down my back was so hot, I shivered. Kol leaned down to kiss me. The moon was so bright that night, I couldn't help gazing out the window. Kol pulled me closer and closer. My legs relaxed as I felt his hands travel down my belly.

He felt so good. He held me tight, controlling every move with ease. Kol pulled me up and down, slowly and softly. I could feel every inch of him tickling my body, but I wasn't laughing. He stopped and looked into my eyes. "I love you," he said.

He picked me up out of the tub and took me to the bed. "Get on your hands and knees," he told me, kissing the lower part of my back. It drove me crazy. He licked the center of my back, and I tingled when he slid inside me.

There was warmth between my legs, where my love had already started to run. Kol gave me all of him. I felt his love with every stroke, and I wanted more than I could take. He made love to me.

"Are you okay? You're out of breath," he said. I told him I was fine, just overwhelmed. I was amazed at how he felt inside of me with his touch. I didn't know it could feel like this.

Kol turned me over, lowered his voice, and spoke to me. His bright hazel eyes darkened as he stared at me and stretched me wide open. My eyes were locked on him as if he had hypnotized me. He went deeper and deeper to the softness of my warmth. I had already cum and I was about to again, then I stopped him and pulled him down closer to me.

"You always make sure I get mine, several times before you," I told him. "Tonight, I am making sure you are completely satisfied." I pushed him up as I kissed his chest and slid under his body. I ran my hands down his back.

I pushed him down and when he sat down, I did too, right on top of him. My back was to him, and my legs opened wide on the outside of his. I leaned back and pulled one of his hands to my chest, and he put the other on my clit. As I motioned around on him, his fingers motioned as well. I had sensations tingling from every molecule in my body.

Heat radiated off of him. I arched my back and he nuzzled my ear. I could hear him clearly. It was like a growl. His arms ran across my chest, flicking my nipples one by one. His wet lips were on the back of my neck. He held me tighter and tighter, and I knew he was about to come. I leaned forward and begin to bounce up and down, up and down, up and down.

He groaned so loud as he burst inside of me. I rolled around, making sure I had gotten every morsel of it. As he began to relax, I slid off him. He was somewhat still aroused. He raised his head up and looked at me with raised eyebrows, and I just smiled since he had already come once, I wanted to make it happen again. I grabbed his dick and pumped from the bottom up.

He started to expand in my hand. As I leaned in to kiss his lips, I felt more and more of him in my hand. I sucked his bottom lip and gave it a little tug. He pulled me down on him, sucking my nipples, tugging on them. He flicked his tongue around them with small bites in-between. I bounced down on him, as hard as I could, but as slow as I could, but it was so hard to control myself.

"Sam, yes, baby," he growled. "Fuck me!" As he commanded, I placed my legs down completely on the floor for more support and put my mouth on his. He opened to let my tongue explore and I moaned.

I leaned back and pushed my waist to him. I put his hands on my ass and motioned for him to pull me forward. "Kol, Kol, Kol," I moaned, falling forward with my arms around his neck and started to rock on him. I pushed my ass down, and his dick was in my throat, or so it felt like it.

He gripped my ass with one hand and my breast with the other one. "Baby, Sam, I am about to come," he said. "I'm about to come."

"Come for mamma, and mamma will come for you again!" I told him. I could feel his soul pass through me. Finally, we were back to breathing normally and laid beside one another.

"Round two later," he said.

I will give it up to you all night if you want it," I told him. "Kol, I want you every day, of every second, of every minute, of every hour."

It was about 2:00 a.m. when I woke up and I was so hungry. I looked over and Kol wasn't there. I went out into the den, and he was there watching Sports Center.

"Hey baby," he said, "did I wake you?"

"No, is everything ok with you?" I asked him.

"Yes, I was just thinking about us and the life we are starting together. A new baby!"

"This is too fast I know," I said before he could finish. "I wanted to spend some time alone with just us before we had kids.

I wanted to travel a bit and just have you all to myself for a while. You know, we don't have to have this baby. It's decision we can make together."

"Sam, what are you talking about?"

"Maybe you want to wait on the baby, wait until later?"

"Sam, you're crazy, have you lost your mind?" Kol asked. "No. I would never ask you to do something like that! I want

our child! There is no way I would give this up! I already love
this baby. I don't know how big this little person is or anything
about it, but I know I love this child. I won't give him or her
up for anyone, not even you."

"Hold up, it's my body," I said.

"I don't care," he replied. "Do you understand what I am
saying to you? I want this life with you. I was thinking of how
much my life is about to change for the better with you and
our son or daughter… in a good way. This is a blessing, Sam."

"I'm sorry, baby," I said. "I didn't mean to upset you." It
got quiet between us for a minute. "How do you already know
you love this baby?" I asked.

"Because I want it, and I usually get what I want." When
he said this, I had to laugh. He gave me a kiss. "Wait," he said.
"What are you doing up?"

"I was hungry," I admitted.

"Let's get you something to eat then." He got me
something, and we went back into the den to watch sports
center. We laughed and laid all over each other. I was in pure
Heaven! I don't even remember falling asleep or getting back
in bed, but when I woke up, I was.

I could smell steak, eggs, pancakes, and coffee. I got
straight up.

"Kol, what are you doing in there?" I asked.

"I am taking care of my baby after all that work you put in
last night," he answered.

"Work? Boy, what are you talking about?"

"You wore me out last night."

"Whatever! If I did, you wouldn't be up cooking. What time is it?"

"About 11:30 a.m."

"Why did you let me sleep so late?" I asked.

"I didn't know you had any early appointments to get to today," he said.

"It's the day after Christmas," I almost screamed.

"Yeah?" he asked. He was not getting it.

"There are sales everywhere," I said.

"You're kidding, right?"

"No, Candy should have called me already."

"Oh, she did, and I told her you were still sleeping. She didn't say anything about it, just to call her when you woke up," he said.

"Oh, well, I guess I will have to catch her another time.

"Give me a kiss!" Kol whined.

"Is that all you want this morning?" I asked, slyly.

"Don't temp me."

"Kol, baby, you know all of this is yours whenever you want it, anyway you want it," I said.

"Damn, I love it when you let me have my way."

"But first, let me eat because if we are going to have a repeat of last night, I should get some more protein to keep up with you."

We ate, made love again, and finally got out in the streets. We hung out and shopped most of the day. Kol bought all kinds of baby stuff, but I wanted to wait. We got to end of the mall, and Platinum Jewelers was in the corner.

"Let's go in," Kol said.

"For what?" I asked.

"Just to look."

We went inside, and the owner was well acquainted with Kol. "What's up, man?" he greeted. "Are you back for more?"

"Yea," Kol said, "this is my Sam. The ring I got last time was for her."

"It looks beautiful on your hand," said the jeweler.

"Thanks," I replied.

"So, man what do you need today?" the jeweler asked.

"Nothing much," Kol said. "I wanted to get a bracelet for my baby."

"Kol, stop it," I said. "You have already given me so much, just take a break."

"Sam, I'm going to do whatever I want, so you take a break," he said.

Another guy come from the back, He and Kol were speaking like old friends.

"I guess you have gotten quite a few things from here then?" I asked.

"Yeah," the guy answered, "Kol comes in all the time with his mom and sisters. They all fight with him not to buy them anything, and they all lose."

"You may as well join the club too," said the jeweler. "Tell me what do you like?"

"I don't know," I said. "You have so many beautiful things."

"Kol, what would you like to see on her?" the jeweler asked. Kol thought for a moment.

"This bracelet to match the ring," Kol said.

"That would be too much," I protested. "The ring is already huge and adding a bracelet to it would just be too much. "That's why we insure everything," said the jeweler. "Don't worry about it. This will be perfect for you."

I couldn't lie, I did like the bracelet. "This is beautiful, absolutely beautiful!" I gushed. "I can't believe how lucky I am to have a man like you in my life. You are so good to me." "Sam, you deserve the best, and I am going to spend my life giving it to you."

"Thanks baby. Now, let's get some dinner. What do you want?"

"You and that's all," he said, looking dreamily into my eyes.

"Be serious, boy!"

"I am. Let's get home right now. You are so beautiful, and you are glowing."

When we got home, Kol got me out of the car and carried me to the door. I opened it and couldn't get my coat off fast enough. We made love in the den. Enjoying sex this much should be a crime.

"I need some rest," I told Kol. "I have a doctor's appointment in the morning."

"Don't you mean we have an appointment in the morning?" he asked. I made a face.

"Candice is going with me since it's her doctor."

"You don't want me to go?"

"No, that's not it at all. If you want to go, you can; it's not a problem."

"Okay, then I'm definitely going."

"I just thought about something!" I exclaimed suddenly.

"What?"

"Maybe we shouldn't have had that last round."

"Why, Sam?"

"Because I will be getting an exam, a full exam, and I hope there aren't any leftovers of your love inside me." "If he is a doctor, I am sure it won't be the first time he has come across it," Kol said.

Chapter Eleven

"I don't want to get out of bed," I mumbled.

"I know, baby," Kol soothed. "We can come straight home after we leave the doctor's office if…. Sam, do you mind if we stop by my office before coming back home?"

"No, why would I?"

"I just want to make sure in case you had something planned after the appointment."

"Yeah, like I'm going to run around in the city without you," I said with a laugh.

"What does that mean?" he asked.

"Nothing," I answered. "I just don't know my way around well enough to be let loose."

We finally made it to the doctor's office, and Candice was already there.

"What's up, Sam?" she greeted.

"Nothing, girl, thanks for coming," I said.

"Anything for my niece," she said, beaming.

"Kol, did you start this?" I grumbled.

"No, he didn't. I just want it to be a girl."

When my name is called, Kol and I followed the nurse to the back. Candice waited out front. Kol held my hand as we walked to the examining room.

"My name is Abby," said the nurse. "I will be assisting today. Let's check your blood pressure, temp, weight, and get some blood."

"Ugh, I hate needles," I groaned.

"Oh, it won't hurt, I promise. It looks like your pressure is a bit high, but not much. I'm sure the doctor will take a closer look.".

The door opens, the doctor walks in.

"Hi, Ms. Smith," the doctor greeted warmly. "I am Dr. Wallace, please to meet you. How are you feeling today?"

"Nervous," I said. "This is Kol Martin, my fiancé." He smiled brightly.

"So, you want to confirm you are pregnant, right?"

"Yes, we both have had morning sickness, and it's horrible," Kol said.

"If I am not pregnant, then something is seriously wrong with both of us," I added.

"Okay, it looks like Abby took your pressure already and a blood sample," said Dr. Wallace. "It should be done shortly. I will go and check on the lab work."

"Kol, why are you smiling so hard?" I asked him.

"Because we are about to bring in a new beautiful life into our family," he answered.

"If it's a girl, you are going to be so hard to deal with, ugh!" I said.

"Why would you say such a thing, Sam?" he asked.

"Because you are already overprotective of me. If we have a girl, you're going to be unbearable."

Soon, the doctor returned. "Ms. Smith, Mr. Martin, you are indeed pregnant," Dr. Wallace said excitedly. I went numb for a minute. I couldn't believe it.

"Kol, what's wrong?" I asked. I wasn't the only one who'd gone silent.

"Nothing," he said. "I am so happy! Candice, what are you doing back here?"

"I just heard Abby say the results are in," she said, "so I followed her. Well?" Kol just smiled and my face said it all. "Oh my God! I am so happy for you guys. I knew it."

"Now that the party has slowed down, Ms. Smith, you will have a lot to do to keep you and the baby healthy," said Dr. Wallace. "I am prescribing a few vitamins for you to make sure you guys are getting all of your nutrients. Also, your pressure was a bit high. Do you have a stressful job?"

"I don't start for a couple of weeks," I answered.

"Just set an appointment to see me a week before you start and two weeks afterward. I just want to make sure you are okay," said Dr. Wallace.

"Thanks, Dr. Wallace. I promise I will take good care of her," Kol said. "She and my baby mean everything to me, and I won't let anything happen to either of them."

"Wonderful," replied Dr. Wallace, "and Candice, please stay out of trouble."

"Okay, Doc, thanks for seeing my girl today," Candice said.

We headed out and I felt so, well, I don't even know. I was at peace, and that was strange.

"Sam, we have to make sure you are not stressed out about anything," Kol said, interrupting my thoughts.

"Kol, don't worry. I will be fine. I have always had borderline high blood pressure," I told him.

"Let's go shopping," Candice jumped in. "I want to get so much stuff for my new niece."

"Candice, stop it. I am only a few weeks, so let's take it easy with all the shopping."

"I promise I will call you later, Candy," said Kol. "Sam are you hungry?"

"No, I am fine. Don't worry. I don't need to eat every hour you know," I said. "Didn't you want to go by your office?"

"Yes, I will only be a few minutes. I have some quick stuff to do, and the paperwork is in my office," Kol said.

"Okay, I will just stay in the car."

"No, Sam, cold as it is. You will come up to my office with me."

"Are you sure?"

"Yes, baby, besides, everyone already knows you. I have a picture of us on my desk."

"Kol, what man does that?"

"A happy one; let's go."

When we got inside, I couldn't stop asking questions.

"This building is huge," I said. "How many floors is it?"

"I don't know, maybe 40 or so."

"What floor is your office on?"

"The 10th floor."

"That's really high up. I hate heights, Kol."

"Don't worry, I got you."

When we got out of the elevator on the tenth floor, it started.

"Good morning, Mr. Martin," said every single one of his employees.

"Morning," Kol said to each person as we made our way to his office. He said it so many times, it made me dizzy.

Kol's office was huge. It had a beautiful view of the lake front.

A man barged in behind us and said, "What's up, man?" to Kol. "Oh, excuse me," he said when he saw me. "I didn't know you had a client."

Kol laughed. "I don't. This is Samantha."

"Oh, I recognize you from the photo. My name is Kris, how are you?"

"Good, thanks for asking," I said.

"It's good to finally meet you. We thought he was making you up for the longest," Kris said.

"What?"

"Yes, he is always talking about you, and we said she can't be real."

"Wow, that's funny," I said with a smile. I thought all was going well until Alisha walked in.

Are you freaking serious? Where did this bitch come from?

"Good morning, Kol. I see you brought your little pet to work today," Alisha said. *This bitch!*

"Alisha why are you in my office?" Kol asked.

"Well, Kol, we do work for the same company. Oh yeah, you know because you got me the job. I bet you didn't tell country grammar that," Alisha said.

"It's time for me to get to a meeting," said Kris. "I will get with you later, man." He walked out the door.

"Look, Alisha, no matter what you do, nothing will happen between us," said Kol. "I'm going to marry Sam. She's already carrying our child, so I would appreciate it if you would leave and not upset her."

"Carrying your child?" Alisha yelled. "Kol, you never wanted a child with me. I can't believe you would do this to me. By getting this bitch pregnant, you have crossed the line, and I will never forgive you!" With that, Alisha stormed out of the office.

"Baby, I am so sorry," Kol said, putting his arms around me.

"Kol, you should have told me she worked here," I said.

"I know I should have told you, he admitted, "but I just didn't think about it. The last time we saw her, it was kind of hectic, and I haven't given her another thought."

"So, you have to deal with her everyday like that?"

"No, she works for another manager. She just comes over to this side to irritate me."

"Everyone else in the office knows about your past with her?" I asked in disbelief.

"Most people just know we had a brief relationship at one time and that is all."

"Kol, besides the obvious, why did you break up with her?"

"Wow, so many reasons and so much drama. She never got along with my family and that is something that I won't give up. Alisha is vindictive and has a bad mean streak when she wants."

"What about the kid's part? You must have loved her at some point, and you never wanted children with her?"

121

"She fooled me for a brief minute," Kol said, "and one day, I saw the crazy. I knew then she could never be in my life forever. Once I really looked at her and how she was, I made the decision to get her out of my life."

"Oh, well, we see that didn't work out at all."

"Sam, she is not our concern, period. You and the baby are everything to me. and that is all I am concerned with."

"Okay," I said. Kol, if you don't mind, I would like to go home. I am a little worked up and I just want to relax. Are you done?"

"No, but I can take you home and work from there."

"Kol, if you have to work, I can drive home. I can use the navigation. Do you want me to come back and get you later?"

""No baby just go home. I'll have Kris drop me off at home."

"Well, as long as Alisha doesn't bring you, I am okay with that." He made a face when I said that. "I'm just kidding! I love you, Kol, and I will see you later."

"I love you too, baby. Be careful."

Well, ain't this some shit, I thought. *I can't believe she works here. What kind of mess is that? And to think, I was considering working with him! I wonder if this is what he does? She did say she watched him with other women, and he always came back her.*

What was I thinking? How could I let that bitch get in my head like that? I didn't have to worry about Kol. *Snap, this hoe is getting on this elevator with me. Out of all the elevators!*

"You think this thing between you and Kol will last, don't you?" Alisha said. "He always comes back to me, baby or no baby, bitch."

"Who are you calling a bitch? You better leave me alone, girl," I told her.

"Let me say this, you can enjoy him for now, but – wait a minute. Did you lie about that baby –"

"You know what, hoe" I cut her off. I couldn't take listening to all her crap anymore. "I have listened to all I will from you, Alisha. No matter what you think, Kol never trusted you enough to have a baby with you, and that was straight from his mouth." She opened her mouth wide, but I pressed on, moving closer.

"I bet he always protected himself when he was with you. Was he even sober when he slept with you?"

"Oh, he was –"

"I'm talking," I snapped. "I don't appreciate you coming in here, telling me about my man. That's right – mine! I have the ring and the baby here to prove it. Alisha, I understand you want him, but trust and believe me when I say I will hurt you about my man! I think I will go relax now in our home, you know, the one he *never* shared with you. It's in your best interest to get off at the next floor because if you don't, you may not make it off alive."

Alisha was so stunned she didn't seem to have anything to say. The elevator dinged, and the doors flew open.

"I suggest you get your ass off and have a great afternoon," I said, and she hopped to. I couldn't wait to get home and call the girls to tell them about this shit!

When Kol made it home, I was still on the phone with them, but I hurried off, telling them my hubby made it home!

"Hey baby, hey! Did you have fun?" Kol asked.

"Yeah, I have been home all this time," I told him.

"Are you serious?"

"There was a small delay when I left your office. Alisha got on the elevator with me, and I had to give her ass the business," I said.

"What the hell was she thinking? I am going to have that ass fired!"

"Kol, baby no. She doesn't mean that much to us."

"I refuse to allow her to pull us into her sad dream. We won't play her game," Kol said.

"Let's not talk about her anymore. I have been plotting all day about how to make you pay for her mess."

"Baby, I'll do whatever you want. I'm sorry about the drama with Alisha."

"Ugh, don't say her name. Let's forget about her!"

"Damn, she really got to you, didn't she?"

"I just don't know what to do to make her understand. She has been just a pain! I have never seen anything like this before," I said.

"Everybody has someone they break up with, and she is just straight crazy!"

"Okay, change of subject: my blood pressure. Remember we talked about me staying home with the baby for a while?"

"Yeah, is that what you want to do?"

"Well, I do want to talk with my new manager first," I said. "I mean I did accept the job, so I don't want to just leave. I think you owe me that much since you brought me in all this crazy ex stuff."

"Sam, if you like it, then I love it. You can stay at home as long as you need to, I do owe you that. Damn, I got some good stuff!"

"What?"

"I must, for you to just go along with anything I say. Ha, I am the best." I punched him playfully on the arm. "I'm just playing, baby," he said "I can be a mess with myself sometimes. To tell you the truth, Sam, you do have the best heat I have ever been inside!"

"Kol!" I swatted his arm again.

"What, you started it."

"I didn't."

"You are so crazy."

"I may be, but I am telling you the truth. When I am inside you, I am lost. That's just some plain ole' good ass heat! If dudes here knew how good that southern loving is, there would be more plane rides to the M!"

"You are so silly," I said, "and I love you for it. You always know how to make me laugh."

"So, you wanna go out to dinner tonight or what?"

"I hadn't thought about it," I said.

"What would you like?" he asked.

"Omelets."

"Are you craving crazy stuff already?"

"No," I told him, "remember when I got up that morning, and you were making omelets? They were really good, that's all."

"Okay, omelets it is," he replied.

"You should stop letting me have my way so much. A girl could get use to this treatment."

"I can't help it, baby. I am a man in love and I would go to the ends of the earth for you and our family," Kol said.

Chapter Twelve

"Kol, we haven't talked about one subject that is not optional for me," I said.

"What is it?" he asked, perplexed.

"We need to talk about a church home. I love being in God's house. He has blessed me so much, even when I don't deserve it. Look at what He has done just for us in such a short time. If He doesn't do another thing for me, I am satisfied because I can never thank Him enough," I said.

"I am so happy to hear you say that, Sam. I was going to take you to our family church this weekend because I can't thank Him enough for you," Kol said. "I know that without God in my life, I would have missed you and our baby. This makes me love you even more, baby! What would you like to do tomorrow, Sam? We can do anything you want."

"I want to stay home all day in bed with you."

"Well, I spoke too soon. I can do half of that," said Kol. "I have to go by one of the shops in the morning, but after that, I am all yours."

Kol was up and out early the next morning. My day was open, so I decided to go see Candice at the shop. I had the time to get a little pampering in before Kol got home.

When I arrived at Candice's for a stress-free day, more drama had come my way. I couldn't believe it. Alisha was in the shop. *What the hell is going on?*

"Candy, can I speak with you please?" I asked Candice.

"I know, Sam," Candice grumbled.

"What in the hell is she even doing here?" I asked.

"I hate to tell you this," Candice said, "but her stylist, Bria, moved here about six months ago. We had no idea, of course. You don't know what kind of clientele you will have with a new stylist."

"I understand, Candice. Do you think Alisha put her up to working her?"

"Alisha is a sneaky witch," Candice agreed, and I bet she told Bria to come by and see me. Although I am sure it was all a setup, I must admit, Bria is a bad chick. I can't hold it against her that she has one client that is a fool. I even get her to hook me up sometimes. Her clients are always on point when they leave the salon, and she comes with a loyal clientele. She is not taking new customers by the way, so don't ask. Anyway, I am sorry, sis!"

"If this trick doesn't stop looking at me, I am going to go off on her again," I said. "I mean, I just may have to give her a nudge this time."

"No, Sam, you must think about the baby. You can't let her get to you, just know that you are the one that Kol loves and there is nothing she can say that will change that. He wanted a family with you, not her."

"I guess you're right, Candice."

"Did Kol ever tell you that Alisha once tried that trick on him?"

"No, he didn't. I mean, he said there was something that really made him realize how crazy she was, but he didn't go into the details."

"Well, she tried to say she was pregnant, but my brother knew she was lying because he always used protection with her. He knew something wasn't right, so he didn't trust her at all."

"Candice, I have no idea why he trusted me. He asked me if I would ever hurt him, and I swear I wouldn't."

"She never made him feel safe, Sam, or that she was really in love with just him. Alisha knew who Kol was and everything that could come with being with him. You are so different, knowing nothing about him or anything about our family. You love him, and that is enough."

"I hope you're right, Candice."

"I am right. This chick has no power, and don't give her any by responding to her. She is nothing to us, nothing to our family."

"Ok," I agreed, "let me get out of here before I have to replace the glass in your shop," I said with a laugh.

"No, don't leave. Just stay and let her watch what she doesn't have. I will call Kol and tell him to swing by," said Candice.

"Candy, that is so awful, but I am so in."

A woman came over and Candice introduced us. "Hey Andrea, this is my soon-to-be sister-in-law, Sam. Could you squeeze her in for glam hands and a pedicure? I'll start on her hair afterwards."

The entire time Alisha couldn't stop looking over to see what we were doing. I followed Andrea to get my nails done. She had her own nail shop connected to the salon. It was called Andrea's Nailtique, and it was busy! I had been following her on Instagram, and I am so glad I came by. She was from New Orleans and had a flair that was unmatched. I would be one of her loyal customers from now on.

"Andrea, can I have the next spot?" Alisha asked as we passed.

"Sure," Andrea said, "in four weeks. I am all booked up, and Sam just got a cancellation. Sorry, Alisha, but if you will be in New Orleans in the next week, I can get you in there."

She was so freaking mad! I loved this, and Alisha was steaming. "Can you believe this heifer stayed at the salon the entire time?" she asked. "Her excuse was that Andrea might have another opening."

Kol walked in with a "Hey, baby."

"Hey, my love," I said, and it took all I had not to jump up and climb that mountain right there.

"Candice has you looking beautiful, sweetie. I swear you become more gorgeous by the minute," Kol said. I could hear Alisha telling Bria something, and I just couldn't stop laughing. "Baby, what is so funny to you?" "Nothing, I was just having a flash back," I told him.

"Candice are you done with my girl?" Kol asked.

"In a minute Kol," Candice said.

"Why?" I asked.

"I want to take you shopping," he said.

"Kol, I don't need anything," I said.

"Well, I just want you to have everything you want."

Alisha was hostile now! "You let that man go?" I overheard Bria tell her. What in the hell did you do to him? With a man like that, it just had to be you cause we all know you a little coo-coo!"

"Shut it, Bria!" Alisha screamed at her, and I loved every moment of her show. For a split second, though, I did feel guilty for rubbing it in her face, but then it was over.

"Kol, do you like Sam's nails?" Andrea asked him.

"I love them," Kol said. "I haven't seen anything like it before." Andrea was great.

Kol leaned in to give me a kiss, and I took full advantage. "Baby let's go," he said. "I think I want to skip shopping and go home. I want to get some alone time with you." Kol had the biggest smile on his face as his eyes darkened.

"Don't you mess that doo up," Candice yelled. "Oh, well, I guess you can come back tomorrow if you need too."

"He led me outside to a jeep. "Wait," I said, "I thought Kris was dropping you off?"

"I had this one in the parking garage," said Kol. We left my car at the shop and headed home.

"Kol, I just want you to know how much I love you," I said. "You are more than I ever expected out of this life, and I can see our love just growing beyond measure."

"I love you too, Sam," he said.

"How much do you love me?"

"Are you questioning it?"

"Are you going to answer the question?"

"Why? What are you up to, Samantha?"

131

"I want some fries from McDonald's and a chocolate shake."

"Are you serious?"

"Yes, I am, I want it, can we go get it?"

"You are a mess. Yes, we can get it for you. Is there anything else you want while we are out?"

"No, I want to lie in your arms when we get home though," I said. We went through the drive-thru. "I love these fries hot!" I squealed.

"Sam?"

"Yes?"

"I love it when you are hot," Kol said.

"When you say things like that, it makes me even hotter," I told him.

"Let's get home now because I want my tongue to go across every spot you got."

"Damn, Kol, you really know how to get a girl going."

"Can you believe we are going for our seven-month checkup?" I asked Kol. "I am so glad you allowed me to stay home until the baby is born, Kol."

"It wasn't a problem, baby," he said.

"You have no idea how much I am enjoying carrying your child. I guess I was freaking out about starting the new position, and I had no idea. I am so glad I kept that appointment with Dr. Wallace."

"That's what doctors are for," Kol replied. "We all want to make this process as stress-free for you as possible."

It was true, I felt no stress at all, only love. "I can't wait to get home and see mom and the girls. I am so excited about the baby shower, too. There's so much to do. Kol, it will be hot in Memphis, so I'm bringing some shorts and sundresses.

"Sam, will you check on the flight times for tomorrow?" he asked.

"Yeah, but why? Are you going somewhere?"

"No, I want the itinerary for you. Send it to my google account, so I can track your flight. You are in the last trimester now, and I just want to take care of you and my son."

"Your son!" I snorted. "How do you know that?"

"Because, baby, I can feel it."

"Before, you just said a healthy baby."

"A boy carries high, and –"

"You have been talking to your mother, haven't you?"

"Let's just get to the doctor's office before you fly out and make sure everything is fine."

"Hey, Dr. Wallace. How does everything look?"

"Sam, you and the baby are doing just fine. He is growing perfectly."

"He!" Kol yelled. "Sam, I told you he was a boy. Baby, you have given me the best gift I could ever hope for."

"Dr. Wallace, I can't believe you just blurted that out."

"Sam, I am so sorry I spilled the beans on that one," Dr. Wallace said.

"Kol is going to be jumping around here like a kid all day," I said. "I can't believe you told."

"Baby, I have got to call everyone and tell them," Kol said.

133

"You should just call Candice and tell her. That way, the word is bound to spread like wild fire."

"You're right."

"Between Facebook, Instagram, Twitter, and Snapchat, it's a done deal. Her news feed will read: Kol Martin and Samantha Smith are having a boy."

"We have got to have a party for the announcement."

"Kol, did you forget I am flying out in the morning for Memphis? You are making plans, and I won't be here unless you want to have it when I get back?"

"Okay, new plans. I am going with you now."

"What?"

"Yeah, I am not going to leave my son to chance; son sounds so good to me. Can you hear daddy in there, Chase?"

"Chase? Who is Chase"?

"Our son, of course."

"What are you talking about?" I asked. "We haven't picked out a name because we didn't know if the baby was a boy or girl."

"Now we know, and I would like his name to be Chase," Kol said. I was so stunned I didn't have a reply. He carried on, "I guess I better call the airlines and book another flight then."

"I have no idea what I am going to do with you," I said.

"You are going to love me until the day I stop breathing, Mrs. Kol Martin."

"Yes, I will," I said.

"The flights have been booked. Let's go home and get me packed."

We landed in the M-Town, and it was so good seeing the big M as we flew over. I was so excited; I was about to burst open. I had already called the family and told them Kol was coming with me. Not a soul minded that he was tagging along; they all had grown to love him.

"Mom! I have missed you so much," I yelled the second I saw my mom.

"Samantha, you are so beautiful," she said, holding me tight.

"Yeah right, you can say big because I have been eating everything in sight," I said.

"Sam!" The girls screamed all at once. I looked up and they were all running towards me. They encircled me, and we smiled without saying a word, tears falling.

"Is anyone happy to see me?" Kol finally asked.

"Silly boy," my mom said, "give mama a hug. You are so spoiled. You know we all are glad to see you, but my baby is home, carrying her first baby. I am so proud of you two." Kol hugged mom and gave her kiss on the forehead. "Don't be giving me that forehead kiss," she said.

" Go on then, mama," he joked.

"You all are coming over to the house, right?" she asked.

"Of course," I answered. "Kol, I have been waiting to get back home to see everyone."

"I never knew how badly I wanted you to come home until you did," said my mom. "I love you."

"Baby, what time is the shower tomorrow?" Kol asked.

"It's at 2:00, why?"

"Okay, I will make myself scarce until the shower is over," he said.

"You don't have to leave," I said. "You can stay. The girls are bringing their men, so you wouldn't have to leave. You all can get to know each other since we will be seeing them soon anyway."

"Seeing them soon, where?"

"At the baby's birth and at the wedding, dummy. This is so much fun, seeing everyone. I have missed all of my friends so much. Just being he makes me happy, and I want you all to know that, Kol. Chase and I appreciate you being a part of our family."

"Who's Chase?" Charese asked.

"Chase is our son, it's a boy," I told them.

"Omg, a little man, I bet he will be so handsome," Charese said.

"I can't wait to meet my grandson. My grandson! My heart is so full Samantha," my mom said. "Kol, I love you so much for giving my baby the gift of life with my grandson. Thank you for loving my baby the way you do."

"Mama, you are going to make me cry," Kol said. "I appreciate everything you have done for us, for allowing me to love Sam and take her away so soon. She is truly a joy and my all."

The girls did a wonderful job for the baby shower. We all had so much fun, and it took hours before we even opened the gifts. The guys had a wonderful time, and it looked like all was well.

Chase had some beautiful gifts, and my mom was without words. I looked into her eyes and I began to cry.

"Sam, baby, what's wrong with you?" she asked.

Kol came in from the kitchen. "Baby, what is it?" He asked, but I could barely speak. I was filled with so much joy and love I was about to lose it. I couldn't believe how lucky I was, to have grown up with such a loving family.

"Mom," I said, "you are the best example I could have had in my life growing up. Girls, you are the sisters God blessed me with. I am so blessed to be here with you all and to have this life growing inside of me. I wouldn't have been anywhere else in the world at this very moment."

"Samantha, please stop crying," Kol said.

"We all love you and feel the exact same way," Charese said.

"I think I love you a little more, though," Kol added. "You are the mother of my child, and I will forever be grateful. I admire the woman you are. You are everything I ever wanted out of life and more. I guess it doesn't hurt that you have a great mom and awesome friends too."

The day finally wined down, and it was time for bed. It felt funny, like I was in a different place. I hadn't been home for a while, so being in my own bed felt funny.

"That's because you aren't home," Kol said. "Home is back in Chicago with me."

"This is still my home," I disagreed, "and it will always be. I love Chicago, but Memphis is it." The house smelled clean even though no one was staying there. It looked great. The girls had done a great job taking care of the place, but I still couldn't fall asleep. I kept replaying the day over again. I couldn't stop smiling, and my man was right there next to me.

Chapter Thirteen

Morning had arrived, and I could smell breakfast!

I wandered into the kitchen. "Kol?" I said.

"Yes, baby?" Kol answered.

"When did you go to the store?"

"Oh, I went a few hours ago when you and Chase were sleeping."

"Why did you get up so early?"

"After a while, I couldn't sleep. I am just so surprised sometimes by the life I have with you. I don't know why. I told you that I would do all I could to make you happy, and I meant it."

"Baby, you are so good!"

"Yeah, and don't you forget it."

"Look at me, Kol?"

"What's wrong, baby?"

"I am huge. This boy is killing me. I am eating so much it's... I have gained so much weight. Just say you still love me even though I look horrible?"

"Sam! You are absolutely gorgeous. Why would you even question the way you look? I love every inch of you from the top of your head to the bottom of your feet."

"Okay, but you must admit, I look awful, all big! There is nothing good about the way I look right now, and you know it."

"Sam, what is wrong with you? Why are so moody?"

"I don't know, I think my emotions have me acting crazy."

"Just eat something and you will feel better."

"Eat something? See, you want me all fat and unattractive, don't you?"

"Sam, where is this coming from? Why are you so upset? It's only 9:00 am."

"Kol, I am so sorry, baby. I just feel like... I don't know how I feel right now. It's like I look at myself, and I am looking at someone else. Nothing fits; I had to buy all new cloths and everything. Even my favorite shoes don't fit anymore. Noting looks good on me. Nothing!"

"Baby, I must say that you in nothing looks pretty good to me."

"Kol, stop it! You are trying to make me feel good."

"No, I'm not. Do you have any idea how beautiful you were the first time I saw you? When I looked at you, you almost stopped time for me. You were breathtaking then, and now that you are carrying our child, you are even more beautiful than I ever thought you could be. You beam beauty, and I see the sun in your eyes every day when I wake up next to you."

"Kol, do you really mean that?" I asked.

"Sam, I am overjoyed when I look at you, and I can see our future in your eyes."

"Kol, stop it, you are making me cry."

"Sam, don't ever doubt how I feel about you or how beautiful of a person you are, inside and out," he said. I ran over to hug him and kiss him with tears rolling down my face.

He brought me so much joy. I still don't know how I lucked up and got that beautiful man. Kol wiped my tears away so softly, and his touch was so gentle to me. He really loved me, and I saw it, I saw it clearly. We sat down for breakfast, and it was so good.

"Who would have thought you would be this good of a cook?" I asked, playfully. "I just love it when you wait on me hand and foot. I am so spoiled."

"Baby, what are we doing today?" he asked.

"I don't know. I guess visit a few friends and go downtown tonight. I have missed it so much. I want to go to Sounds of Memphis; Gerald will be singing."

"Can he sing?"

"Are you serious?" I asked, like he was crazy.

"Baby, I have never heard of this Gerald. Gerald who?"

"Kol, Gerald Richardson can *sang*, not sing, but sang! I haven't heard him in so long. It is going to be great."

The day went by fast. We visited both of my grandmothers. It was a delight to see them both. They are nothing alike.

Madea, my mom's mom, she is 82 years old and still has the entire neighborhood scared of her. Kol laughed the entire time at all the stuff she said. If you want to laugh, she has got you.

Bea, my dad's mom, is totally opposite. She is quiet, and she smiles at everyone. She is mild-mannered but makes the best burgers and fries you will ever eat in your life. I was blessed because they both are beautiful and amazing in their own way.

We stopped and got lunch. I knew we would get something to eat later at the club, so I didn't want to overdo it.

When I got dressed and looked in the mirror, I could hear Kol's voice telling me what he thought earlier, about how beautiful I was. I had to admit in my new dress, I looked about five months instead of looking seven. I was surprised my son wasn't killing my shape like I thought.

I did still look pretty good, as Kol had said. I was so excited to hear Gerald sing again. We jumped in the car and went down the 240.

"Is there a lot of smoke in the building?" Kol asked, sounding worried.

"No," I told him. "People have to go to the outside back door to smoke."

When we got there, I wanted to sit upfront and hoped a table would still be available.

"Let me out, so I can get to the door," I said. Tamara greeted me when I walked up, and she gave me the biggest hug!

"Where in the world have you been?" Tamara asked. "Tiffany told me you left town." We caught up a bit up until she saw Kol coming across the street.

"Hold up, girl," Tamara said, "I have got to say hello to that man coming this way."

I quickly stopped her. "He is with me," I told her.

"What the hell?"

"Tamara, this is Kol Martin, my fiancé," I introduced.

"What, where, who, and how did I miss out on this news?" Tamara asked.

"Kol, this crazy bird is Tamara. She has been here as long as I have been coming, and I must say, nothing has changed," I said.

"How did you snag this one?" Tamara asked. "Hey, your ass has gotten bigger. He must be taking good care of you, hunty!"

Smiling, I said, "Yes, he is, along with our baby boy, who we will have in two months!"

"Oh shit! I am so happy for you. Let me seat you, and I will tell Gerald you are here."

"Sam, what in the world have you gotten me into? And why does this Gerald need to know you are here?"

"Nothing, baby, nothing," I said.

It was time for the show, and Gerald hit the stage.

"Good evening, everyone!" Gerald said into the microphone. "Are you ready to have a good time?" The crowd said yes! "Well, you came to the right place tonight. This is going to be an extra special night. My old partner, Sam, is in town tonight."

"Sam, what does he mean partner?" Kol asked.

"Honey," I said, "Gerald and I use to sing together for a while."

"You never told me you sang? I know you sing in the shower, but you actually use to sing, like professionally?"

"Yes," I answered, "I just don't do it anymore, that's all. My voice changed, and I never liked it after it did, so I just stopped singing except at home."

"Wow, I am about to marry you, and I had no idea. What else are you hiding from me?"

"Nothing, I promise, fingers crossed."

Samantha," Gerald said, "I am going to sing your favorite song." The keys started, and I knew it was Donny Hathaway's "A Song For You." I loved this song, and when Gerald started to sing, Kol had to admit that he was mind blowing.

Gerald did a few more sets that had the crown going, some Johnny Taylor, Marvin Gaye, and Earth, Wind, and Fire.

"Sam," Gerald said after finishing a song, "Would you come up on stage and sing with me?"

I was nervous. I hadn't sung live in so long, but I got on stage anyway. "Gang, it's been a long time, and I hope I don't disappoint you," I said. "Let's give Sam a big round of applause," Gerald said. "Now, we're going to sing another favorite." The music started, and it was Womack and Womack, "Baby I'm Scared of You." The crowd was up, and Kol was looking like, *who is this woman?*

When we finished, I went back to my seat as Gerald continue to woo the crowd. Kol gave me a big kiss.

"How could you hide that side of yourself from me?" he asked.

"I wasn't hiding it," I said. "I was just going to surprise you later with it."

143

"You did," he said. "You shocked the shit out of me. Were you planning on singing at our wedding?"

"Oh, no, I will be crying way too hard for that."

Gerald finished his set and came over to meet Kol. They shook hands, and Kol told him how amazing he sounded. Gerald was so humble.

"Thanks, man," Gerald said. "It's nothing I did by myself. It was all by the grace of God and the gift that He wanted me to have." We ordered a round, of course a virgin for me!

As we are sitting, I heard Tiffany on stage, announcing it was time for karaoke!

"What? When did you all start doing karaoke?" I asked.

"About six months ago," said Gerald, "and it's a hit."

"You will hear some good stuff and some horrible stuff," said Tiffany, "so enjoy! Alright, our first singer is visiting from out of town, the windy city! She is singing a hard one, ladies and gentlemen, Natalie Cole's "I'm Catching Hell." Give a round of applause for Alisha!"

"It can't be, Kol!" I hissed. "It is her! What is this witch doing here?"

"She must have followed us, but how and when did she even see us? "

"Who cares how she did it! I am about to pull the bitch off the stage and just kill her," I said, getting up to confront her. "I am so tired of her stalking us and our family. This is it, Kol. She has crossed the line. Who follows someone out of the state just to stalk them?"

"Let's hear it for Alisha from Chi-town" Tiffany said.

"Bitch," I said, "how dare you come to my town with this shit? I am going to fold your ass up!"

"Sam, stop it," Kol tried. "The baby!"

"Kol, is this who you want to be the mother of your child?" Alisha asked "Someone who jumps to conclusions at any time. You do know, Ms. Sam, that the Memphis Moon isn't just for you. I visit Memphis quite often for your information."

"When have you ever visited Memphis, Alisha?" Kol asked. "You have never mentioned anything like that when we were…"

"Say it, Kol, when we were together," Alisha said.

"Look Alisha," I butted in, "trust me, I understand how you feel, but you don't have this man, *my* man, anymore. He is everything and more, but you didn't get it right, and I did. I trust that this will be the last time we meet this way, or you will regret it. I promise that because right now, I am going to walk away from you, just like Kol did."

"You're a bitch, Sam Smith! I hate you! Be happy for now because Kol will never forget about me, I will make sure of it!"

"Alisha, get this through your head," Kol said. "I don't love you. I never did, and I never trusted you. I don't even like you as a person anymore. You are disrespectful, selfish, and just plain crazy with all the games you have played."

"Kol," she said. "You don't mean that. It's that witch. She's done something to you; let me handle her!"

"Alisha, If you ever threaten my wife and child in any way again, I swear I will kill you."

"But Kol, you have never said anything like that to me,"
Alisha said. "You don't love me at all?" I thought that maybe
she was finally seeing the light, but then, she stepped to me
again. "Sam, this is your fault, and I promise you, I will –"
Smack!

"Whore," I said, "I am going to kill you, myself. Now, if
you want some more, just keep standing there! I am about to
stomp a mud hole in your ass." "You just stepped way over the
line, Sam. I promise, Kol left me for that bitch, and she will
pay! "Alisha yelled to the onlookers. "I won't let her have him.
If I can't have him, she can't either! Everything was fine until
she showed up. He's always came back, but now, she will pay
for this!" We could hear Alisha screaming as we made our way
out the club.

"Can you believe that bitch?" I asked Kol once we got to
the car. "She actually came here of all places! Not in my town,
that shit just ain't gonna happen!"

"Sam, you should calm down and think about the baby,"
Kol reasoned.

"Kol, he will be fine; it's that damn Alisha that won't make
it."

"You need to stop thinking about her, remember she is
nothing to us," he said, trying to calm me down as he drove.
"She has no effect on our future. Baby, it's all about us and
nothing else. Chase will be here soon, so you can't be all
stressed out, making him come too early."

"It feels so good to be home," I said as Kol pulled into the
driveway. "I could use a drink."

"Sam!" Kol gasped.

"I know I can't drink, but one would be so good right now, especially after what just happened, but instead, I will take…"

"If you want, I can make one for you." All virgin?

"That doesn't sound good at all, Kol. I want a tropical margarita right now."

"I will see what I can do, Sam. he said. "It looks like you have plenty to mix. Damn, girl, were you an alcoholic?"

"Shut up and just make the drink, like now! Was that rude?"

"Yes, Sam, that was very rude."

"I'm sorry. Come over here, so I can give you a hug and you can feel how sorry I am." He walked over and wrapped his arms around me. "I think this is much better than the drink, baby. You feel so good. Kol, promise me we will always be together." Sam, there will never be anyone, but you today, tomorrow, and forever," he said. "Thank you for standing up for us." We heard a loud crash.

"What the hell was that?" asked Kol.

"I don't know," I said. He looked out the window.

"Sam, baby, your car!"

"What about my car?"

"God, it's on fire!" Kol yelled. I nudged him aside to look out the window.

"Look at that bitch standing there. Alisha is right there. This is it. She's on my property, and I am about to shoot this bitch."

"I'm calling 9-1-1," said Kol. "Don't worry; everything will be ok."

"Yeah, you call them. I don't give a fuck about my car; I am on my way outside to shoot that whore!"

"No, Samantha! You can't go out there, it's too dangerous."

"You don't understand do you, Kol? She came to my house to threaten me; shit, she set my car on fire; and I am supposed to do nothing? Not fucking happening!"

"Baby, the fire department will take care of it."

"Is that bitch still out there?" I asked. "Is she? Dammit, answer me, Kol!" The police arrived. I flung the door open and flounced outside.

"Baby calm down please. Just come inside and sit down. You shouldn't even be out here!"

"Really, I shouldn't be out here?"

"No!" Kol yelled, pulling me back inside.

"She shouldn't be out here, and I will make sure she is never anywhere else again." "Get back in the house, where it's safe NOW!"

"She is good as dead when I catch her! I am gonna make her wish she were never born. You attack me at my home when I am pregnant and endanger my child!"

"Sam, what is wrong with you?"

"Look, Kol, I have always taking care of me when I needed to, and I am about to take care of this situation now!"

"You sound insane, Sam!"

Suddenly, a sharp pain ran up my spine. I grabbed onto the door frame for support. "Kol! Something is wrong with…" I managed, but the pain is so strong it hurts to talk, "…the baby! Oh God, my water just broke!"

Chapter Fourteen

"Sam!" I heard Kol yell. He called for the firemen to come into the house and help me.

"How far along is she?" asked a fireman.

"She's seven months, almost eight," Kol answered.

"Please save my son," I cried. "I don't care about myself!"

"Calm down," said the fireman, "We are going to take care of you. My name is Derek, Derek Haynes. Demond, come help!" The second fireman, Demond, brought over a case with medical equipment in it.

Kol was almost hysterical, telling me he loved me and needed me.

"It looks like we are going to have an early baby," said Derek.

"No, it's too early," I said. "He won't…"

"The ambulance is on the way," Derek said. "Don't worry, just focus on the baby. I need you to calm down and breathe. Concentrate on your son. I need you to do exactly as I say, okay Sam?"

"Yes, I will do anything," I said.

"Okay, ready? You're gonna push now. We need to get your son out and to the hospital," Said Derek.

"Kol, please help me," I said. "I don't want him to die."

"Sam, I am gonna need you to push!" Derek yelled.

"Baby, push, we are going to be just fine, push!" said Kol. "Sam, you are doing just fine."

"Push again, I can see the head," said Derek.

"Sam, baby, keep going! I can hear the ambulance! I'm going to meet them," said Kol.

"No, Kol, don't leave me, I need you please!" I yelled. "God, this hurts so bad, Kol! So much pain, I can't push anymore!"

"Okay, baby, I won't go anywhere," said Kol.

"Sam, push one more time! Give us a big one," said Demond.

"Ugh," I moaned. "Kol, Kol, the baby, why isn't he crying?"

"Sam, he is beautiful and smiling," Kol said. "Sam, he is fine!"

"Okay, everybody," said Derek, we need to get you and the baby to the hospital right now."

Demond stayed in the back of the ambulance with us while we were transported to the hospital.

"My son, how is he?" I asked.

"Despite how early he came, this little guy looks good," said Demond. "He is clearly a fighter. The doctor will let you know how well he is when he looks at this guy."

"Thank you so much," I said. "Thank God for you, Demond, and Derek."

At the hospital, it felt like it took forever for the doctor to see us. When she finally walked in, I was on pins and needles.

"Ms. Smith, Mr. Martin, your son is just fine," the doctor said.

Kol and I both let out sighs of relief. "Are you sure he's okay?" asked Kol.

"Absolutely, he's doing very well."

"Oh my God, Kol," I cried.

"You are also doing well, despite your high blood pressure. All I can say is you must have been doing exactly what your doctor told you because your son is doing better than most premature babies born this early. We, of course, will be keeping an eye on him for the next couple of weeks and you too. Try not to overdo it. Right now, he is being monitored and is in very good hands, so get some rest. I will be back later to check in on you."

"Kol, can you believe it?" I asked when the doctor left. "Our son will be fine. I love him so much; I had no idea how much I did until I thought we would lose him."

"I know, Sam. I'm so thankful. I'm happy you both are okay," said Kol.

"We have got to call mama, the girls, and Nell! God, we came for a shower, and it looks like we will be in Memphis for a while now. Will that work with your work schedule?"

"Sam don't worry about that now. Don't worry about anything. Baby, I am just glad you are okay. I thought I was going to lose you and Chase for a second."

"I know, Kol, I'm sorry."

"Sam, that was the scariest moment I have ever lived through. You were willing to just die if Chase was ok. I am so happy that I will have you both forever."

"Kol, I will always be yours until the day I stop breathing. Let's go see Chase now."

"You should be careful now. I don't want anything to happen to either of you."

I took Kol's advice and settled down. I was drifting off to sleep when my mom walked through the door. "Mama!" I exclaimed.

"Baby, I am so happy you and the baby are ok," my mom said, giving me a big hug. "When Kol called me, I almost fell out! Where is my grandson? He is in the NIC unit resting and doing fine."

"Sam, baby, I don't want you thinking about that right now," said Mom. "I need you to concentrate on getting back home and taking care of Chase."

"Mama, I'm trying."

"Ok, I will let you rest, and we can talk about all this mess later. Can I go to see the baby now?"

"You can look through the glass for now," said Kol. "You can't hold him yet, ok?"

"Mama will be right back," she said. "Kol?" she stopped and asked.

"Yes, mama?"

"Can I get you something, son?" she asked him, and he shook his head, no. "You are a Godsend, the way you have taken care of my baby girl. I can't tell you enough how much I love you for it."

"No thanks needed, mama. Sam and Chase mean everything to me, and I love you too, just in case you were wondering. I'm fine, I don't need a thing," said Kol. My mom left, and Kol's phone started ringing.

"It's Candy," he said to me and answered. "Hey sis. Everything is fine. No, you don't have to jump on a plane right now. No worries, they are fine, I promise," he said and hung up.

"Jesus, I had to promise Candice I would buy her something just to keep her home for now," he said.

"Did you talk to your mother yet?" I asked.

"Yes, she is glad you are both ok. I told them all to just wait until next weekend to come down, which will give you some time to rest."

"You already know how they are," I said. "They will be all over you, and we know how that worked out last time. Charese!" My friend walked through the door and gave me a hug.

"Sam! God are you ok?" she asked.

"Yes, I am fine, and Chase is doing well."

"Friend, I am so happy for you. I couldn't believe it when Kol called me and told me what happened. That bitch is…"

"Charese, stop now!" Kol interjected. "I don't want Sam thinking about any of that right now. I just want her to be ok and get through this."

"Kol, honey, I am thirsty. Can you see if I can get something to drink?" I asked.

153

"I will be right back, baby," he said and ran out of the room.

"Ok, now, listen quick, Charese," I said. "Alisha is in town or was. She followed us last night to Sounds of Memphis, and then back to my house and set my car on fire! That is what sent me into labor early. I am going to kill that motherfucker! You can't say a word when Kol comes back in ok?"

"Right, just get better, and we are going to whoop this bitch!" she hissed.

"Sam, I checked, and all I could get for you right now is ice cubes," said Kol, returning. "They will check with the doctor to see when you can eat something, too."

"That's fine. I think I want to get up and see Chase now. Charese, will you ask the nurse if it's ok?"

"Sure, be right back," said Charese.

"So, when is the rest of the crew coming?" Kol asked.

"I don't know. They have all called and said they will be here ASAP. It will be crowded in here soon."

"Sam, the nurse said it's fine, we can see Chase now. I am so excited!"

"Kol we can see our son!"

"Mama hasn't come back yet! What do you think she is doing down there?"

"Who knows? She is probably trying to take pictures through the glass."

"But on a flip phone?" I asked.

"Look at him; he is so tiny," I said. "My baby, oh my God, I am so thankful that God spared his life. I promise I will give anything up in the world just to be near him. How could I have been so stupid; I almost lost him."

"Sam don't say that. It wasn't your fault, baby. You did nothing wrong, it was that damn… Just wait and see how dead she will be."

"What did you say Kol?" I asked.

"Nothing, nothing, baby. Look at Chase. He is doing so well."

"Ms. Smith, hi," We shook hands. "My name is Teka." said one of the nurses. "I'll be taking care of your son. He is a beautiful boy."

"Teka, I'm glad you feel that way," I said. "I will be so excited the day you tell me we can take him home."

"It will be one day soon, ma'am. A strong boy like him won't be here long."

"Teka, please let me know if anything with him changes. I don't care how small it is, just let me know. I'm going back to my room now," I told her. We made our way back to the room, and I got settled into the bed.

"Baby, I am going to check with the nurse and see if you can have anything other than the hospital food, I will be right back," said Kol.

"Kol," said a voice I had become too familiar with lately.

"Alisha," Kol said.

"What the fuck are you doing here?" I asked.

"No, Sam, I'll handle this," Kol said. He grabbed her by the arm and dragged her out of my room.

"I had to come by and tell you how sorry I am for everything," Alisha said from outside the door. "I never wanted to hurt you. You have never been angry or hurtful towards me. You have always just forgiven me, and this time when you spoke to me like that, I just lost it. I thought that if I couldn't have you, then they couldn't either, but I know that was wrong."

"What the fuck is wrong with you!" Kol yelled. "If you don't get your ass out of here, you will need a room before the police can come and get you. You better run far and hide because Sam is the only thing saving you right now."

"Kol, I just want to apologize to S–"

"I don't want her dealing with you anymore. I'll deal with you. Leave, and when I find you, I am going to kill you slowly. I am going to torture you for every moment of pain you gave Sam, for thinking she would lose our son, for thinking I would lose them both."

"Kol, I've never seen you this –"

"No, Alisha. You wanted me to want your ass, and right now, I do. I want to kill you and leave nothing to be found. Whatever family you have left won't be able to identify your body. Don't say you're surprised. You knew this me; you always said you never wanted to meet this me, but you fucked up, didn't you, Alisha?" he asked.

She was crying so hard; I couldn't make out anything she said.

"Stop crying," said Kol. "You will need that energy to run, to hide, and mostly, to pray."

"Kol," she said, "nothing happened. I only wanted to scare her, and that was all. I–"

"You what? You scared her so bad, she went into labor. You put my son in danger, and for that, I can't ever forgive you."

"But —" she tried.

He cut her off, "You will have a head start to get out of here. You better find a hole to crawl in because as soon as I can, I am hunting your ass down like the bitch you are. Now, get the fuck out of here before I change my mind and just kill you here and now."

The door clicked and Kol walked in slowly. "Babe, what's wrong? What happened?" I asked.

"Oh, nothing, honey, I was just thinking."

"About what?" I pressed.

"Nothing to worry about," he answered. I was proud that Kol handled Alisha the way he had, but it scared me. There was another side to the man I loved with all my heart. It made me feel safe and protected, but also, it worried me.

Weeks later...

"We're home, Chase, well to one of them," I told the baby. "Do you like it?"

"Samantha, of course he likes it," answered Kol.

"Baby, will you make sure you get all of his things in the den. I want to make sure we have everything. I have a list."

"I am sure you do have one," Kol grumbled.

"What's wrong with that?"

"I can't mess up at all, not even a little."

"Because of my temper, I put our son in so much danger, and for six long weeks, we couldn't bring him home. I couldn't bare it if something happens because of me, so I keep a list to keep myself from overreacting to things.

"Sam, it's okay, and Chase is a beautiful, happy boy. It wasn't your fault. We are not going to talk about this anymore. We have everything, and Alisha is out of our lives for good. She is nothing to us."

"Well, Kol, do you think she will ever come back and try to hurt us?"

"I don't know. She looked pure evil when she was here the last time. I won't let her hurt Chase; I will die first," he said.

"Baby don't say things like that!"

"Trust me, I have it handled."

"Kol what do you mean you have it handled?" I asked, remembering the conversation he had with Alisha in the hospital.

"Look, don't worry about it. You need to focus. Chase is a preemie, and he is doing well, but you have to just worry about him. Alisha won't bother you –us anymore."

"Okay, Kol. You're right."

"Baby, I must fly back to Chicago later this week. I have been away from the office for too long and need to go back to sign some documents. I have put it off long enough, but I have got to go do this."

"Baby, why didn't you tell me sooner? I have everyone here with me. Kol and I will be just fine. You could have left long before now."

"Sam, I couldn't leave you after what happened. I hate to leave you now, but duty calls."

. "When are you leaving?" I asked.

"I must fly back by Friday."

"That's in two days."

"Well, I guess that will give you time to miss me," he said.

"You know, I already had my six weeks' checkup, right?"

"Doesn't that mean we can…"

"So, when you get back, I will be waiting on you."

"Why do we have to wait until I get back?"

"So, you will miss me more!"

"More?" Kol asked with a large grin. "It's been a minute, mama, and you know how much I crave your touch. It's been pure torture not being inside of you. You haven't even let me feel your pussy; I couldn't kiss it or anything. For me, it's been so hard having the other little man locked up like he is in prison."

"Kol, stop it," I said. Kol walked behind me and kissed me right behind my ear, whispering please as he slides down to my neck. His arms were around me, pulling me closer and before I knew it, I was on his lap. I felt how long and hard his little man had gotten!

He took my mouth, kissing me like he had been starving. Oh my God, the things that man could do with his tongue. My mouth and tongue relented to him. I allowed him to take me, and I was breathless when he released me.

The look in his darkened hazel eyes told me what he wanted and just when I was about to surrender, a loud cry came from just to the right of us. Chase wasn't having any of it!

Chapter Fifteen

Kol

"I just landed, baby, and I am missing you already," I said on the phone. "I will get back ASAP. Take care, and I love you."

"Is Kevin still picking you up at the airport?" Sam asked.

"Yes, he is here now. I gotta go, baby. Kiss my man for me." I hung up with Sam, and dabbed Kevin. "Kevin, what's up man?"

"Nothing, Kol, why did you come back for this?" he asked. "You know I would have handled it for you."

"I just wanted to get this taken care of myself and get back to my family. I didn't want anyone else involved. I'm not taking any chances. Alisha needs to know what she almost cost me, and who I almost lost. I almost lost my life and my love fucking with that bitch."

"I hear you, man," said Kevin.

"I need her to know that this shit is unforgivable before she takes her last breath."

"Kol, what are you planning on doing?"

"Kevin, I can't tell you that. I don't want anything traced to anyone. Alisha has got to understand that there is no way I can let her get away with this."

"Kol, you know I got you, bro. You have done so much for me, but man, you have too much to lose. You have Sam and Chase now. I have come to love Sam as my sister. I don't want you to be apart from your family, especially with everything Dad did to us!"

"Kevin, I know, but I have to do this," I protested.

"Don't get me wrong, I love our siblings, but did he have to do it like that to mom, make her suffer through the shit he did? How many women would've stuck by him while he was locked up? Mom stayed through it all, even with all the shit he did."

"Kev, that's different –"

"Do you want to relive that with Samantha? Mom loved Dad with her all, and he just had to ruin it with all the affairs, baby after baby. I mean, how long did he think Mom was going to take that shit? Now, look at him! He misses her, but he is alone. Sometimes, he talks about how Mom was the love of his life, and he messed that up. He feels guilt, trust me on that. You don't want that Kol; don't do it."

"Kevin, I would never do Sam like Dad did Mom. I would never cheat on her. I love her with everything. As she breathes, my heart beats in sync; we are one. She means so much to me that I can't think straight."

"Then, think about her and don't do this.

"I know it's wrong, but Alisha went after Sam and my baby. I can't let this one go, Kevin. I only have this one thing on my mind from morning to night.

"Sam makes me a better man, everything I wanna be she makes me. I had no idea what I wanted until Sam walked in into my life that Saturday. I thought I was just going to enjoy a game in Memphis, to check out the band, and nothing more.

"Samantha Smith changed that. She makes me think about everything now in a new light. I wonder how it would affect her before I make any decision now; she means that much to me. I want her to be proud of the man I am. I just don't know what she would do if she ever knew who I was before her.

"What do you think she would say about the old Kol, the one I am right now? The back in Chicago ready to end another person's life? How do I explain that to the woman I love, the mother of my son, and the woman I will marry?"

"Kol, every one of us has a past, even her. She has got to know that you may have been someone else?"

"Kevin, I don't know if she can understand what I have come from, and if she can handle the things I have done to become the man she loves today, what if Sam doesn't understand? What will I do then? I can't imagine the world I would have to live in without her. She may not be so understanding, and I can't take that chance. I love her too much, Kevin, and I won't be able to live without her. If she leaves, she takes Chase with her and that I won't jeopardize"

"Kol, I am about to play both sides, so hear me out! What if Sam told you she used to sell ass? She was a high-priced whore. What would you do? Could you forgive her? What if she told you she just passed herself around to the highest roller because there was a new player on the scene?

"Could you honestly say that you would be ok with her being the woman you want to marry, mother of your child? If she did, you know it's too late now, right? Kol, you should think about this. What are you going to tell her about your past?

Has she ever asked about what you did before?"

"No, Kevin, she hasn't asked, and I don't think it matters to Sam now."

"If that is what you think, bro, then tell her the truth, the whole truth. What will she say about the ruthless Kol Martin that I know and love, the dude that is willing to do anything to save his family?

"The man that is willing to give up everything to protect the ones he loves? You risked so much for us. You are the oldest, and you said from the very beginning of this life we ran in, that there was noting that you wouldn't do to get us to a better place.

"You were a sinister motherfucker while you were in school! How the fuck you pulled that shit off, I will never know. One minute you were in business class, and the next, you were beating the shit out of a cat with a Louisville Slugger bat!

I thought you were going to kill that dude on the south side ally by Walgreens when he fucked up Mike about that weed. Man, you lost it, and the whole time you were wearing a Polo set with icy white kicks."

"Man, we use to get into some mean shit," I said.

"If you love Sam like you say you do, then you should let her know what and who you are. You can't let any surprises come out. She doesn't know anything, and if someone approaches her, then what? You have to," my brother pleaded.

"Kevin, I am not sure about it. I mean, Sam is a different kind of woman. Most of them whores back then loved me for that shit. They loved the meanness I had in me. Sam has only seen my sweetness, and she gave it back to me. She's only been sweet, kind, and loving. She has never showed one ounce of a mean streak, well, except that night she went into labor. She was on another level that night!

"Alisha was trying to hurt us, and she lost it! I have never seen that side of her, Kevin. I wanna say for a second, she was insane. I had never seen her like that before. I know we haven't been together for that long, but I never expected that," I said,

"When you start messing with money or family, you just don't know how that will turn out," Kevin said. Trust me, Kol, you should just be honest with her. You haven't even gotten married yet. What if some shit just comes out during the wedding?"

"Look, Kevin, I feel you, but this, I can't do. They are too important to me, and I just can't risk it."

Sam

Since Kol was out of town, I had a chance to do some research.

"I hate this," I told Charese. "I said I would never go back to this again, but after Alisha, Charese, I must."

"Samantha, you can't be serious?" Charese asked in disbelief.

"Samantha? Charese, you haven't called me Samantha since…"
I shook my head. "Look, Alisha stepped over the line and crossed it twice. I can't wonder if she will strike again. I must

protect Chase and Kol." Don't' you think you are moving too fast? And besides, Kol Martin was a grown ass man the last time I saw him. She isn't stupid enough to stay in town, Sam. You should wait for everything to die down," she said.

"You said it, Charese, die. I'm going to kill her."

"I think you are going down the wrong road with this one. Sam, I am going to call Kol if you don't stop talking crazy like this."

"Charese no, I don't want him involved in this," I said.

"How can you say that, Sam? He is already involved! It was his fucking ex-girlfriend."

"Look, you are getting out of control. Sam, just wait, you are doing too much! Your son was barely born, and you are here conniving and forming a plan to kill someone. What the hell are you going to do if someone finds out?"

"So, you are really going to call Kol? Damn, Charese, you would tell him? I don't get it! We were some ride or die chicks back in the day. If you messed with one, you got us all on your ass at the same time."

"You are right there, Sam, but we were teenagers then. We didn't have families that depended on us then., We thought we had nothing to lose. I know you remember when we got pulled over that night, right? After we set that guy's garage on fire... with him inside of it! We smelled like gas and smoke. Luckily, we got pulled over by Tammy's dad.

"He never asked or said a word, did he? I wonder how Todd looks now. He deserved to burn for trying to rape Lindsey! We would have never gotten out of that shit if it wasn't for Tammy's dad, and you know it! Sam, we did some horrible stuff to people, and by the grace of God, we never got caught. I am here to tell you, Karma is still a bitch, no matter how much time has passed!

"Sit your ass down. Be happy you have a beautiful son and a man that loves your stupid self unconditionally. We all have waited, Sam, for someone like Kol to come along and sweep each of us away, and you got it! He is a good man, the definition of what all of us wanted, so don't be a bitch and blow it. Be happy for once!

"No more looking over your shoulder again. Do you remember how that was? We had to struggle to come up out of that shit, to completely turn our lives around! No one knew the real shit we were into. People just assumed we were good girls because we had nice things. That night life was nothing to play with, the one we chose.

"We all said that when we were out, we were out! Don't go back on that, Sam, not to satisfy this crazy rage you have for this second. Know what you have with Kol, know that Alisha has nothing. I won't forgive you if you mess this up. I promise I will tell Kol the entire truth about the real you if you push me."

"So, you would just rat me out Charese?" I asked. "Just like that, you would do it?"

"Sam, I would, and it's because I love you. We have been friends for so long and protected each other from so much. when we get in our own way, one of us must protect us from ourselves, and that is what I am doing now!

"Just answer me this, because you are a grown ass woman and I won't ever mention this conversation again: are you willing to lose Kol and Chase forever? If you are, then I won't say a word. If you are ready to give up the life that you have had with them so far, and you are ready to give up any happiness you may have in the future, then I won't say a word.

"If you are ok with Chase growing up without a mother and his father hurting every time he looks at his son, then I won't say a word."

"Charese, do you know how much I hate you right now? I haven't been that angry in so many years. It just all came back so fast, like it was just waiting to come out. The bitch in me is always lurking, waiting on something to jump off. Charese, thanks so much for being here, for being my friend!

"I almost convinced myself it was the right thing to do. Damn, I went down that road fast with no seatbelt on. I went from 0 to 60 that fast. I must have been out of my mind; I don't know what I was thinking.

"Kol left for a few days to check on his business, to make sure our lives are comfortable, and here I am, plotting to end it all. I am so stupid. What was I really going to do though? I mean, my God!

Charese, girl, I love you and thanks for being here. I am so glad you didn't slap me like the last time I went off the rails.

"You deserved to have the hell slapped out of you, though."

"I know, but what would Chase have thought about you slapping his mama?"

Chapter Sixteen

"I hope Kol is ok," I said. "I haven't heard from him today."

"Of course, that clown is good, Sam!" Charese said. "You are just mad he isn't here to hang onto your every word."

"Yeah, you're right, I am. I have gotten so use to him being by my side. With him gone, I just don't know what to do with myself," I said.

"Well, there goes Chase," Charese half-screamed over Chase's bawling. "He must know you are talking about his daddy. You better stop it. He is getting really loud! Go get him out of the bed; he needs to feel one of you."

"My darling Chase," I said once I picked up the crying baby. "Your mamma is a basket case. I just about lost my mind for a second. I was about to ruin our family, but thanks to your Teetee ReRe, I am back to reality. Oh, he just needs changing and a bottle with his greedy self."

"See, look he is already falling back to sleep," Charese said.

"Let me give your daddy a call since you are sleeping," I said, dialing Kol's number. "Baby, what are you doing? I haven't heard from you all day. I miss you so much."

"I miss you too, Sam. What is Chase doing?" Kol asked.

"He is back down for a nap. He must have known I was thinking about you. Suddenly, he is starting to cry and got fussy. It was like he knew you were away, and I was missing you something awful."

"Aw, I'm sorry to hear that."

"So, did you find out anything with the business? Is everything ok?"

"I am still working on it. That's why I haven't called. It's a lot to untangle right now. I have so much to consider. And just so you know, I will know exactly if Alisha moves."

"What do you mean? How would you even know what is going on with her?"

"Sam," Kol said, "I must know what she is doing at all times. Baby, she tried to take away the most important people in my life, and if you think I will just stand by and wait on her to make a move, you are out of your mind!"

"Kol, calm down; I know exactly how you feel. I was crazy, almost out of my mind earlier. Luckily, Charese was here and clamed me down. Kol, how long will you be gone? I have to talk to you about something."

"What is it?" he asked.

"I would like to talk about this in person. It's about…"

"Sam, has something happened? Does this have to do with Alisha? I am gonna execute that bitch!"

"Kol! No, nothing is wrong with us. We are fine. Kol, what just happened to you? Where did that come from? I have never heard you speak like that before. Please listen, everything is fine, and Chase and I are safe.".

"Sam, I am so sorry I scared you like that. I just got really upset without thinking. I was so worried that she had tried to get you both."

"Kol, who is she really? You are freaking me out right now. Why would you think she could do anything to us now? What kind of woman is she?" I asked.

"Baby, I am just out of my mind because I can't be there with the two of you," Kol said.

"You didn't answer me, is she that crazy?"

"Sam, when I get back home, I will tell you everything. Just be careful, ok?"

"I will, you know I will protect our son. Just try to get back to us as soon as possible. We will be here waiting." I hung up with Kol.

"Charese, he doesn't sound good," I told her. "He sounds nervous, and I have a bad feeling about this trip. He got upset about Alisha possibly getting to us, and he sounded like someone I didn't know.

Kol

"Kol, bro, did you just hear yourself with Sam?" Kevin asked. "If Sam knows you so well, then she has got to know you are flipping out about something. She seems smart, Kol. She will figure out what you are doing."

"Kevin, not a word! I don't care what she asks you; mouth shut, and I mean it.

Sam

"Chase, I know I promised your Teetee I wouldn't do anything crazy, but I just want to find out what is going on with your daddy. I have got to know if he is safe," I told Chase.

"This is for us. I won't set up anything. I will just investigate things. This isn't just business, like your dad said. There's more behind this trip, and I can feel it. He's never not called us back, even when he's super busy. He has cancelled meetings just to see me. I know something is going on, I don't know what!"

God forgive me! I called the number I had sworn I'd never call again,

"Tony?" I said when he answered.

"What's up?" he asked.

"This is Sam."

"Girl, it's been a minute. I heard you moved, got engaged, and dropped a load."

Yeah, you always know what's going on as usual."

"Ok, spit it out, what's up?"

"Tony, I need you to dig up some stuff on a chick from Chicago."

"Oh yeah? That chick you slapped outside of the club a few weeks ago?"

"Wow, you know everything, Tony."

"Sam, if you think I wouldn't keep tabs on my biggest producer and my top-notch bitch, then you don't know me at all, do you?"

"I know, Tony, but that was a long, long time ago, and I really don't want to have that conversation now."

I already have a tail on the girl. Did you know she was at the hospital after you had your son? Look, you did a lot of deals for me back in the day. You were always good with the numbers on supply and demand.";

"What the fuck you mean at the hospital?" Later?

"Yeah, she was talking to yo' dude in the hallway and I think he was about to kill that bitch too. He looked like he was giving her ass the business; she looked terrified. She looked like Twin did right before you blew his ass off."

"Tony! You are spilling too much over this phone, dude," I said.

"Oh, don't worry. If you had a tap, I would know it. Look, meet me at your pop's place, ok? I know you still got it; you pay the mortgage on it every month."

"I will need to get my mom over to stay with Chase," I told Tony and hung up.

It didn't take Mom long to make her way over to my house. I kissed Chase goodbye and whispered, "Mama will be back soon. Thanks, Mom, for coming over to take care of him. I just need to run a few errands, and I will be back ASAP. Love you!"

When I arrived at my pop's place, Tony was there waiting with a smile on his face.

"Hey, Sam," he said, grinning.

"Tony, it's good to see you," I said.

"Damn, you still fine even after that load you dropped."

"Stop it, fool! Tony, I need you."

"I have been waiting to hear that again for some time now."

"I know it's been a long time, but for this, I don't trust anyone else. You were always good to me, and I have no reason to think anything has changed on that level."

"You're right, Sam, it hasn't. What do you need me to do?"

"Kol is back in Chicago. I spoke to him, and I know something isn't right. He sounds different, and I know him better than he thinks I do."

"Ok Sam, what do you need?"

"What do you think I need to do? I trust you; you already know the situation, so what's your plan?"

"I can have a tail on him within the hour. You do know that you may not like what we find out? When you look for shit, you find it. Do you know everything about him, I mean everything? Have you asked about his past?

Have you tried to find out anything and he always changes the subject? Look, I already know what this cat has been into, Sam. Although you didn't ask me, I had him looked into when you brought him home the first time."

"Tony! What?"

"We don't talk, but you are always my concern. You rode with me for a long time, and for me not to know what is going on with you is... You know, you mean a lot to me."

"So that's how you can get a tail so fast? You've already investigated him? Tony, I don't know how I feel about that, but right now, I need to know what he is up to."

"You don't trust him, do you?"

"It's not him; it's her that I don't trust. He is very protective, and I think he will do anything to keep us safe."

Sam, first tell me what you know about his past."

"I just know he has money from his family, some shops here and there over town. He told me about some investments and of course, his actual job."

"What did he tell you his job was?" Tony asked.

173

"He is an executive with AT&T. I've been to his office before; it's nice. I met a few people, and everyone knows him. When we walked in, everyone was breaking their necks trying to speak to him. I thought it was pretty funny."

"Well, that's not entirely the whole truth. There is more to it. What else do you know about his past?"

"Damn, Tony, tell me what you know. That seems better than for you to wait on me."

"I know that he isn't just an executive. He owns a large share in the company. He really hasn't told you anything. Sam, I'm not sure you are ready."

"Tell me everything you know, Tony."

"He came up on the Southside, where it all started. He went from errand boy to the man. Your man has been in some deep shit, but I must say, he had a plan. He started college while he is running a small drug empire.

"He was the ultimate hustler. Hell, I kind of admire the bastard, especially since he has you now. For me to give him his props, he has to be the man. He used his money and his smarts, graduating with honors and getting a job.

From there, he started the first shop for his family. He was smart and didn't move too fast. Sam, the motherfucker is smart and ruthless. That's what you heard in his voice, isn't it? You got worried because of how he sounded, didn't you? You've been around that life before and recognized it.

"You remember it from when you used to run with me. You need to talk to your dude and let him tell you the whole story. This shit is too close; you gotta get the rest from him.?"

"Damn," I said, "I started a life with him, had his baby, and planned to marry him, but I don't know him at all. What the fuck? How much more do you know?"

"Don't act like yo' shit don't stank, Sam. Does he know the real you or about me? He has no idea, does he? How we met, and the shit you use to do for me.

You are about to lose it, and yo' closet is just as dirty. That bitch needs to be cleaned out too. Skeletons and bodies are stacked up. I'm just saying, you can't be ready to pass all of this judgement on his ass, and you haven't thought once about 'Sam, the Pusher to Punisher. That bitch was wild, and I loved her."

"That was different, Tony."

"Was it? Really, how different? Look, tell me what you want me to do, and the rest of the personal shit, yall will have to work out without me. I'm not into this kind of shit, therapist and all, unless…. will this get you to lie on the couch and tell me all your secrets?"

"Fuck you, Tony. It looks like you know all of my secrets and his too."

"I do know all of yours… from the inside out, likes, dislikes, and how you feel on the inside."

"Tony, stop it. Just put the tail on him for now and let me know what's up in about an hour or so. After that, we will go from there. Now, do I get the discounted rate?"

"For you, Sam, this is free. I figured I owed it to you since I had no idea what I had when we were together."

"Tony…"

"Nawl, Sam, don't get all sentimental on me. Just flow with it, you remember how to do that right? I'll holler at you in about an hour, and then you can tell me what you wanna do."

Later....

What in the fuck am I gonna do? I asked myself. *How could I not know? What does he know about me? Does he have any clue who I was, who I am? I don't know what to do!*

Deep breath, I told myself because I had to back to the house. Charese was going to explode if she found out! What was I going to tell her? I promised that I wouldn't do anything

Chapter Seventeen

That was so long ago, a time when I was someone else. I know Tony, I trust him. I have trusted him with my life. Lord, all because I fell in love with a man that another chick is in love with! I just couldn't pick out some random, a normal person from Memphis.

That way, I would know everything about them. Hell, I could have checked him out myself. I didn't know what to do! I was so in love with Kol, and we had Chase! I would marry him no matter what, but I should know everything before I do.

I had to get it together. I needed to get in touch with Kol and tell him the truth. I had to make him understand that I didn't care about his past. I hope he didn't care about mine. I had to tell him that I knew.

Oh my God, Kol would want to know how I found out! He was going to kill me. I was having him followed. He'd never trust me again. When he answered, I almost didn't want to say anything.

"Kol, it's me," I said.

"Baby are you ok?" he asked.

"I was really worried about you when we spoke before. Look, we really need to talk."

"Sam are you ok?"

""Yes, well kind of. We need to have a sit down. I have some things I need to tell you about me."

"Sam, what are you talking about?"

"Babe, it's really a discussion we should have face to face."

"Did you change your mind about us with all this drama, Sam? I am going to kill Alisha!"

"Kol no, where are you right now? Who are you with? It's too late to be at the office.

Kol, whatever you are doing, believe in us! Don't let her win. I know you better than you think I do. I can feel it when something is wrong with you, just like you can with me. Whatever it is, whatever you are thinking about doing, don't! All that matters is us, you, me, and the baby; she doesn't.

Alisha will spin this, and you know it. Some kind of way, she will use this against us. I have been here before, in this place when all you want is revenge. Kol, if you love and trust me, come back to me now. Do you love me enough, us enough, to come back? Are you still there? Say something damn it!"

"I will be on the first flight home to you and Chase," Kol said. "We are moving forward now. When I get back, we are going to pack you up and start planning the rest of our lives."

"I love you!" I said into the phone and told Chase, "Daddy is coming back tonight! We must be ready, ok? Are you going to be a good boy when he gets home? No crying, Chase. You know you broke us up right before he left, so you must be a good boy. Why are you smiling so hard, spitting bubbles everywhere?

In hardly any time, I got a call from Kol.

"Sam, I just landed, and I am 30 minutes away," he said. "I can't wait to see you. I love you, babe, and I will see you soon."

After I got off with Kol, another number sprung up on the screen. "Tony?" I answered. "What's up?"

"I know I was supposed to call you, but it got hot for second. Alisha is back in town. She made some moves, and she is planning to hurt one of you. I got a guy on your house now and a guy at the airport. Your dude just landed and so far, so good. He is being tailed but Alisha is in the wind. This bitch coo-coo for coco-puffs. Before Kol, she spent some time locked up in a nut house."

"What are you talking about Tony? How could no one know this?"

"Because she comes from money, old money, and a lot of it. She has been paying her way out of everything for years. Yall better be careful. I can come by and stay until he gets there."

"No, I have to explain everything already, and you being here will just complicate things."

"My guy just sent a message, saying everything was going well. Just be ready to be the bitch you use to be because I don't know how this will flow," Tony said.

"Mom?" I called from the other room. After I came home, she stayed a bit longer to help with Chase and spend time with me.

"Yes, love," she answered.

"I need a favor. Can you take Chase to your house for the night? Kol and I will be over in the morning to get him. He is on the way back to Memphis."

"I will, sweetie. I love spending time with this little man!"

"Call me when you get home please."

"Sam is everything ok?"

"Oh, yes Mom, we may even come by tonight and get him. Don't forget to call me."

"Everything squared away?" Tony asked, still on the line.

"Yeah, Tony, I just sent my mom away with the baby.

"I know, my guy just saw her."

"I told you not to send anyone over here. Never mind, just tell him to follow and protect them; I will be fine. I can take care of myself." Let me know if you need me there. I would hate for Alisha to get your ass."

"Fuck you, Tony, I wish she would," I said, hanging up because I was getting a call from Kol. "Kol, you should have been here already, what is going on?"

"There was a wreak on 40. You didn't get the update?" he asked, laughing.

"Sam, I am glad you called when you did. I was about to… don't worry. I know we must talk. I love you, and I don't want to have any secrets between us. I will be there soon, my love, to see you and our son. I don't hear him; is he sleeping?"

"No, I sent him home with Mom for a few hours for us to have some alone time. We can go get him later."

"Ok, I will see you in 15 then."

When I saw Kol's lights, I ran to the door and opened it. As he shut his door, I saw Alisha, standing there with a gun!

"Noooooooo," I yelled, but I was too late. Alisha shot him. Alisha disappeared as I ran to Kol. "Baby look at me, baby, please look at me!" I dialed the police.

"9-1-1, what is your emergency?"

"My husband has been shot!" I yelled into the phone.

"Ma'am, what's your location?"

"73006 Emerald Lake. Please hurry, please!" I hung up the phone. "Kol, think of Chase. He is waiting on you to pick him up. Please, baby, look at me. I need you to stay awake."

"Sam, yes baby, I'm here. I won't leave you," Kol said. Blood was everywhere. The paramedics arrived, but I had a hard time letting Kol go.

"Ma'am, you must move and let us work," one of the paramedics said.

"I won't leave him!"

"Ma'am, you can't go past this point."

"Oh Lord! Please help me, please save Kol! Charese was right, this is all my fault for all the shit I did before. Please God, save him, I need him, and Chase needs him. I will do anything, just save him!"

At the hospital, hours passed by, and we hadn't heard a word.

"Nurse," I asked is there any word on my brother?" Candice asked. "We have been here for hours, they flew right in after I get them the news. We need to know something!" His family was there, along with my friends. I had to call my mom and let her know what was going on because Chase would need to stay longer.

"Guys, I need to leave, I have got to get everything my mom needs to take care of Chase."

"Sam, stop crying. I know my son, and he will come back to us all. He loves you so much, and there is no way he will leave you now," Kol's mom said.

"Nell, you are right," I said. "I must be strong."

"Look, I will go with you and stay with your mom," Nell said. "It will make me feel close to Kol, and I can help your mother."

"Candice, call me if you hear a whisper," I told her and left with Nell.

Candice

"Sam Smith!" someone yelled, shortly after Sam left.

"Doctor," I answered, "do you have any news?"

"Yes, who are you?" the doctor asked.

"I am Kol's sister, what is going on? Please tell me his is alive."

"He is, Ms. Martin. Your brother is a strong man. He was shot several times, and if the last shot was an inch to the left, we would be having a very different conversation."

"Thank you, thank you, thank you!"

"He is being taking to recovery, but he will be in ICU until we are absolutely sure he is out of the woods."

"Thank you, Doctor! Thank you, God!" I yelled and immediately called Sam.

Sam

"Candice, what is it?" I asked the second I answered.

"Kol is…" Candice started, but she was crying so hard I couldn't understand her.

"Tell me!" I yelled at her.

"Kol is alive," she blurted. "He is going to be ok. The next 24 hours will be critical, but the doctor is hopeful, Sam. Get back here. I know he will want to see you when he wakes up."

"Thank you, God," I said. "Thank God for saving him." I told Candice to call our moms to give them the news.

When I walked into the waiting room, everyone stood up and surrounded me. I fell into Candice's arms. "He's alright," she said. "He's resting. No one has seen him yet; we all thought he would want you there first."

"Can I go in now?" I asked the nurse.

"It isn't quite time yet," she said.

"Nurse, my soon-to-be husband and the father of my child is lying in there, and he needs to know I am here," I pleaded with her. "I won't say anything; I just want to hold his hand, please!"

She finally gave in and let me go into the room. Hours passed, morning to night and back again. It seemed like I had been in there forever, but I didn't care. I was going to be there when Kol woke up.

"Sam…" Kol groaned and reached for me.

"Kol! Baby how are you feeling?" I asked.

"Chase," he said. "Where is Chase?"

"He is fine, babe, just fine. He is with our mothers at my mom's house. Let me get the doctor."

"No, stay with me. Don't leave my side."

"I promise I will never leave you; I'll just push the button."

"Well, look who is awake!" exclaimed the doctor.

"Doctor, how long have I been out?" Kol asked.

"For five days now," the doctor answered. "I am rather glad you were. It has allowed your body to rest and do some much-needed repair for itself. You should get as much rest as possible, but you will be here for a while."

""How long?"

"We should take it day by day, Mr. Martin."

"When can I see my son please?"

"Your son is small, a newborn, and he shouldn't be here."

"Doc, I need to see my son."

"Mr. Martin, we already allowed your fiancée to be here before and after the time she's allowed."

"Well, what's one more?"

"Give it a week first, and we will go from there. This is all I will promise you," the doctor said before leaving.

"Kol, don't rush it, baby. Let the doctor take care of you, and I will take care of Chase," I told him.

A week later...

"Mr. Martin, you are doing much better, and I think you are up for a visit from a special young man," said the doctor. I entered the room, holding our son in my arms.

"Chase, look at you! So big and happy. I have missed you so much!" Kol exclaimed.

"He has missed you too, baby. We all have missed you," I said. "I can't wait to get you home. I'll cook you a real meal and get you in your own bed."

"Wow, you miss this D already, Sam?"

"Shut up, boy. I am just glad you are ok and alive."

Weeks went by, Kol got better, and life was truly good. Kol took a leave of absence. Things were going well, but in the back of my mind, I never stopped thinking about Alisha! I still had Tony looking for that bitch, but I still needed to tell Kol the truth.

"Kol, how are you feeling?" I asked. "We really need to have that talk soon."

"I am fine, is everything alright?" he asked.

"That depends. Kol, before you were hurt, I was having Alisha tailed."

"What?"

"Kol, once upon a time, I was a different girl with different friends and a very different lifestyle. I had my hands in quite a bit over the years, but it was in the beginning. I am not proud of it. I was lucky, and I got out at the right time."

"Sam, what exactly are you saying?"

"I am saying that I went from the bottom up to becoming the right hand and woman of a very powerful man. Kol, I was into some very bad stuff. I am telling you this because when you left for Chicago, Alisha was being followed by someone for me."

"You what?" he asked.

"What did you want me to do, Kol? She almost made us lose our son, and I just couldn't let that go!"

"So, you make all the decisions now, and you know what we need? Sam, that wasn't fair for you to do that at all! I was taking care of it."

"You? What the hell? Oh, you didn't mean to let that slip out did you, Kol? You said you were home on business, but

185

you went back to find her, didn't you? So, how the hell are you fucking with me about what I did years ago? I came to you to tell you the truth, but you? You were just going to keep me in the dark about the whole thing! Kol, what were you going to do?"

"I was going to have the bitch killed, Sam!"

"You were?"

"Yes, I was because of what she did to you and Chase, to all of us."

"You are nothing like that, Kol! You don't have a dark place in you, and I don't believe you could hurt someone else, but I can. I still have someone tracking her. She is in Detroit right now. I get updates daily, sometimes more than 3 times a day."

"That's a little intense."

"I love you, Kol, with all I am, and she almost took my entire family away. I will kill her for that, and that is what I am willing to do. She shot you! She almost killed you, and you think I am just going to let that shit go? Oh, and guess what? I found out she is mental, I mean, for real mental –"

"I don't give a damn about that."

"Her family pays of the people she hurts, instead of taking care of her. She can't pay me off."

"Sam, you can't be this person. Who are you?"

"I am the bitch that takes care of business, Kol. That is who I am. I gotta get out of here. Take care of Chase for a while."

"Sam, where are you going?"

"Don't worry; I won't kill anyone while I'm gone!"

Chapter Eighteen
Kol

"Kevin, I need to talk to you," I said.

"What's up? Is everything alright?" my brother asked.

"Hell no, I just found out Sam was a hustler. I mean, she was into some deep shit back in the day, and right now, she has someone watching Alisha. She knows where she is and everything."

"Are you serious? How the fuck did you miss that shit? So, you got a ride or die chick for real. Damn, I knew I liked her for some reason."

"Kevin, shut the fuck up! Man, look, this shit isn't funny," I said.

"Where is she now?"

"I don't know. She left out of here like a bat out of hell, and I have no idea where she is or what she is doing."

"Damn, your bitch ain't playing with you."

"Don't call her that!"

"I didn't mean it in a bad way, dude. Calm the fuck down. Look, you better get off the phone with me and find out where the fuck Sam is. Get at you later."

"Sam, pick up," I said, dialing her number. "Baby, pick up."

Sam

"Kol is calling again," I said. I was on the phone with Charese.

"Maybe you should answer it," said Charese.

"No, I don't want to speak to him now. I told him the truth about who I was, and he was too concerned with why I was still tailing Alisha."

"Look Sam, it was a shock. Hell, if I wasn't there, I wouldn't have believed it myself. I mean, who would believe that shit?"

"Whatever, Charese."

"You need to go home, Sam. I'm sure Chase is wondering where you are."

"Really Charese? You pulled the baby card?"

"Look, I have got to reason with you somehow. I know you are upset about how he reacted, but you have got to give him a chance to understand it and get through it. How would you feel if Kol dropped a bomb like that on you? I mean…"

"You mean what?"

"Would you just understand immediately and act like it never happened? You know damn well, you would have a fit for him not telling you about it."

"Well, guess what he did? Kol didn't go back home just for business. He was looking for her too! He had the nerve to come for me. I don't think so. He was too busy being upset at me, and he forgot to check his own self."

"So, what you are saying is you both have pasts, and you are just now discussing them? You are pissed that he knows about you, but now that you know about him, you are mad at him? Just think about it and go home. I am sure he is worried sick about you. He has called a million times. Go home and talk to him! Let him tell you how he feels about everything and get it out in the open. You should give him a chance to listen and understand, and so do you. Jumping to conclusions, yelling, and storming out isn't the answer," Charese said.

"Look, Charese, he was wrong!"

"And what were you, Sam? Go home, bitch and talk to your man."

"Fuck you, Charese. I'll call you later." We hung up, and I clicked over to answer a call from Tony. "Tony, you have something?"

"She is staying in a room and hasn't been out of it in two days," he said.

"I wonder what the bitch is up to?"

"Don't worry; she won't make a move without us knowing."

"Keep me posted!"

"Bet!" After checking in with Tony, I decided to listen to Charese's advice and head home.

"Sam is that you?" Kol asked when I walked through the door.

"Who else are you expecting?"

"Can we just start over Sam?"

"I don't think so. There was too much said and too much done already to start over."

"You have got to understand," Kol said. "I am trying to process this, Sam. I can't imagine you as this person you say you were."

"Well, we did move too fast in the first place. There wasn't time to talk about everything, but I can say the same thing about you, Kol!"

"Not exactly –"

"Who are you? Where were you hiding this, and was I ever going to find out? You flipped out on me, but you had things to hide too. Was it just because you are a man, and I am a woman? You think it's just men who run things?"

"No!" Kol yelled, and Chase began howling.

"Chase is crying. I'll be right back," I said, going to pick him up. "Hey, sweet man, did Mommy and Daddy scare you? I'm sorry, man. Daddy is being a big hypocrite and Mommy doesn't like it."

"Really? That's what you have to say to our son? The one who you ran out on? You got so pissed off at me, you forgot all about him."

"How fucking dare you!" I yelled. "I love this boy more than life itself, and he is the reason why I did what I did. She had to be taken care of, and you were doing the same thing, Kol, without telling me a thing."

"Sam, if you would sit down and let me explain, then maybe you will understand. Are you willing to listen, please?"

"Fine," I said. "I guess I owe you that much."

"Sam, I love you and will do anything to protect this family the only way I know how. I never portrayed myself as a saint, but you did!

I knew a while ago about Alisha's mental state, but it wasn't something I could just talk about on a first date. *How would that go?* 'Hey, I'm glad you could make it. By the way, I have a psycho ex-girlfriend?' When I first left, I was in a rage and wanted to kill her. I didn't want her on the same planet as you and Chase, but then Kevin asked me to think about your feelings?

"The night Alisha shot me, I was ready to come completely clean with you about everything: my past, the person I was before you. I didn't get a chance to tell you.

"I wasn't the runner; I was the motherfucker you use to work for in my town. It was only small time in the very beginning when I was still in middle school. By the time I was in high school and college, I was the man. I put my cash away because I knew I wanted to get my family to a better place.

"I ran my money through several outlets to clean it up. Look, I did what I had too to get my family safe, just like you did. Once I had enough and I had established legitimate businesses, I was out. There's so much more, Samantha, but at this point, do you really want to know who I am not anymore?

"I am the man you love, the father of our child, and the man that you will marry. I am no longer the man that sold drugs and hurt people. I already know where Alisha is. Whenever she flips out, she reverts to the same place. She goes to the hotel where she killed her parents and the brother."

"What?"

"Yeah, she did it a few years ago after she stopped taking her meds, and she thought they were out to get her. Her state of mind has been in and out for years. I wanted to kill her at first, but I know why she's the way she is.

"She was sexually assaulted by her brother, well, half-brother, and no one believed her. Her mother married his father when she was twelve. Dillon started with small things, like touching her face, forehead kisses, and then, it escalated from there to flat out rape.

"By the time her parents realized it, it was too late, and the damage had been done. Her brother had beaten and repeatedly raped her. When her parents tried to help her, she thought they came to find her and take her home for more abuse. She wouldn't listen to reason because she couldn't, and when they approached her, she shot them both.

"She shot them in the same room where she killed her brother, and his body was still there. I know it's no excuse, Sam, but it does have a bearing on it."

"Kol, are you serious right now? She has had to deal with this her entire life? Damn, that's unbelievable. Kol, why didn't you tell me?"

"What was I going to say? My crazy ex killed her parents? My son could have been taken away from us. Look at him, he is so innocent, and there is no excuse, regardless of what her problems are, for what she did."

"Still, that would've been good to know," I said.

"Sam, baby, I am not asking you to forgive her. I am asking you to forgive me. Forgive me for not being honest with you from the very beginning. I just didn't think Alisha would go off the rails like that. She hasn't been this kind of a problem for some time now."

"When do you think it changed for her?"

"When she came to our house, I saw it then, but I was too worried about you and the baby. I'm sorry. I left to try and protect the both of you. I was wrong. Please forgive me. I will do anything to make it up to you and Chase, even if it takes me the rest of my life.

"Kol, I was wrong too. I didn't tell you all about me either. I thought that part of my life was over, and I never had to revisit it again. I had an old contact, and I called him."

"Him? Really?"

"Look, Kol, it's not time, ok?"

"Who is this guy?"

"He is the head of the crew I used to run with," I answered. "He always kept an eye on me, even when I didn't know it. He asked if I needed anything. I was so upset and wanted so much revenge. He just came in when I thought I needed it. You were hurt, and I didn't care how she got taken care of. I just wanted it done. I can call him off at any time, but I don't need to right now."

"I can't tell you what to do, but I can ask for you to just let me handle it," Kol said.

"Why you, Kol? You wanted to kill the bitch, I could tell by the way you spoke to me over the phone. You were so angry, so why should it be your people?"

"Sam, I know you are mad, but at this point, she needs to be placed in a facility. I know you want her hurt, but now you know what she has gone through. Do you think she deserves to be hurt again?"

"You are going to have to give me some more time. I don't quite know how I feel about this! And why are you Captain Save A-Hoe today?"

"I just want to concentrate on our son and be with him now. I don't want to think about her," Kol said.

It was hours later, my head hurt, and my emotions were all over the place! I just wanted some normalcy for a minute.

"Do you think we could get some dinner, Kol?"

I will go anywhere you want," he said.

"I don't know what I want, just surprise me. Will you get some wine, too, while you are out?"

"Yes, I will, and is there anything else you would like me to get?"

"No, I'm fine."

"You are, and I miss being close to your fineness."

"Hurry back, ok?" I asked. Kol smacked me on the butt and left quickly. I grabbed my phone.

"What's up?" Tony answered.

"Hey, Tony, I'm just calling you for an update," I said.

"Well, she is in the same place."

"I know why she is there. I found out some stuff about her."

"I already know, Sam there's a lot about her. She's straight crazy!"

"Yea, I know."

"How the fuck yo' man even hook up with this basket case?"

"I don't know that was before my time."

"So, what you want me to do with her?"

"Nothing yet, I am still thinking."

"What the hell you mean you thinking?"

"A lot of shit happened to that girl."

"So, you are going soft now?" Tony asked. "You had me tailing this bitch for you to think about it? I know you want her gone, right?"

"Look, Tony, this is my decision and not yours! I say what happens, remember? If you have a problem with what's going on, you can always just drop it, and I will have Kol take care of it."

"Damn Sam, you really shooting off on me right now! Look, I can leave the bitch and you can handle it, whatever way you want. I was only trying to help your ass since the bitch was at the hospital ready to finish the job. You do what the fuck you want and have that fuckboy of yours to take care of it."

"Boy, what the hell do you mean?"

"He ain't shit, Sam. If you let him take care of it, I will keep it moving, but if you were still mine, this bitch would have already been in the ground, no questions asked. Peace!"

Chapter Nineteen

"Charese, I have fucked up really bad. Tony is pissed at me!" I told her over the phone.

"What do you mean, Sam? You didn't call him for real, did you?" Charese asked.

"I thought I needed to. I found out some really bad shit about Alisha."

"Who gives a fuck about her?"

"She was raped and abused for years by her brother, and no one believed her. It was too late, and she killed them all. Now, she's staying in the same room in the same hotel where she did it."

"Oh my God, Sam! She went through all of that?"

"That's why she is a lunatic! She got off her meds and is just crazy now. I know what she did, and I hate her ass for it, but I feel bad. Lord, help me!"

"Sam, what did you have Tony do?"

"I had him follow her and keep up with every move she made," I said. "I thought I wanted her dealt with, but I was wrong. When I told Tony to wait, he flipped out on me, talking about I should get Kol to take care of it. He almost sounded like he used to about me. Do you think he meant it, like back in the day? I mean, he said that he has always kept up with me."

"That's not surprising, Sam. He did care about you. Do you really think he has been keeping tabs on you this whole time?"

"Charese, Tony knows about everything that's happened basically since I started dating Kol. He had so many details about the situation."

"Well, look Sam; you know he didn't take it well when you left him."

"That was so long ago though."

"You were his top notch, and he wasn't happy about you walking away."

"I left because I had to leave that part of life behind, and that included him."

"There were always whispers about how he wanted you back."

"People talk all the time."

"Well, some of those whispers said y'all have been back together, but you had to keep it quiet because you had gone corporate. They said you wanted everyone to think you were legit."

"Are you kidding me right now?" I asked her in disbelief.

"No, I have heard it before and the girls have too. Remember how we would go out and no one would approach you? Everyone knew that you and Tony were an item. Nobody wanted to fuck with that. He still has a thing for you, how could you not know it?"

"Because…"

"Because what?"

"I just never thought about it after I walked away."

"Well, you have to deal with this somehow."

197

"Look, I gotta go. Kol is back with dinner," I said quickly and hung up.

"Hey, honey," Kol greeted. "I got dinner."

"Babe, what did you get? You were gone so long."

"Oh, I went to Fleming's. I know how much you like their steaks."

"Did you get the wine too?"

"Yes, where is Chase?"

"He is down for a nap, so we better eat fast."

"No, enjoy it, and if he wakes up, I will get him. I just want you to relax. You have been through so much with Chase and with me, I just want you to know how much I love, admire, and appreciate you. You're the one that keeps me going; your love for me pushes me to be a better man. I would do anything for you, and I just want you to know that I love you today, tomorrow, and forever." Kol, we have a lot to discuss, but know that regardless of what you tell me, I am in this for the long hall. We have a son together; I have never had a child or even contemplated having children until you. You remember how I reacted when I told you about being pregnant?"

"Yes," he said, "you freaked out."

"I will always love you, Kol, and no matter what, that doesn't change. Yes, we have hit a rough patch because of someone from your past, but we have a future together, a wedding to plan, birthday parties, and school functions. We will be solid again. We just have to sort through things."

"Sam, I love you so much," he said.

The next morning, Kol and I went to his doctor's appointment for his check-up.

"Mr. Martin, you have healed wonderfully," said Dr. Johnson. "All of your test results are clear, and your heath is great."

"I have been taking good care of him, Dr. Johnson," I said.

"Yes, she has," Kol agreed.

"He has been on his suggested diet and exercising weekly, along with his physical therapy," I added.

"I am glad," said the doctor. "I wish all my patients followed my directions like this."

"Dr. Johnson, when can I travel back to Chicago?" Kol asked.

"I would like you to see me for one more week. If everything still looks good, I will release you to travel, and you can see your regular physician."

"Baby, you hear that, released!"

"You can take him home now and enjoy the rest of your evening," said Dr. Johnson, and he left.

"Thank you, Dr. Johnson. Sam how long will your mother have Chase?" Kol asked.

"Until we pick him up, why?"

"It has been so long, and I have been dreaming of being back inside of your love."

"Kol, what baby?"

"I have missed you, touching you, having my hands all over you. We haven't made love since before Chase was born, and quite frankly, I just really want to fuck you senseless!"

"Kol! I want you," I said, "and I have wanted you for so long, even before my six-week checkup. My pussy has been aching for you to be inside of it."

Before I knew it, we were home. The entire time I was driving, Kol rubbed between my legs and pinched my nipples. Every once in a while, he'd lean over to kiss my chest. Once we got home, his eyes burned into me, his mouth fell on mine. He kissed me so deeply that he forced my lips apart with his tongue.

I moaned as our tongues collided with each other. I felt a pull between my legs, deep within my pussy. I could feel Kol's dick growing longer, wider, stronger against my stomach. I wanted to fuck him from seven ways to Sunday.

"Sam?"

"Yes, baby?" I asked.

"I'm going to enjoy this," Kol said. He slipped my top over my head; he didn't even unbutton it.

He leaned down to kiss my chest, palming my breasts as he sucked on my skin. Oh God, his lips felt amazing. He kissed farther down until he was on his knees. At 6'4, his mouth was on my stomach. He unbuttoned my jeans, and as he unzipped them, he kissed the outside of my panties. I could hardly keep myself contained. I rubbed the back of his head, pushing it into me. I wanted his mouth on me so badly; I had missed being completely his.

"Please stop teasing me," I moaned. "Please fuck me!"

"No, Sam," Kol said. "I am going to make you want me more than you ever have before, make you beg me to be all over you."

He pulled my jeans down, and I stepped out of them, but left my panties on.

"Babe, what are you –" I started, but he put his fingers over my lips.

"Wait," he said. I took his fingers inside my mouth and sucked. Kol sat me down on the chaise lounge, and the Memphis Moon burned into the room as he unclasped my bra.

Lucky for me, I wore the one that clasps in the front today. My breasts fell out, and his hands were on them, playing with my nipples. Kol circled them, pressed them, and squeezed them. My breath hitched, as Kol kissed my lips again. I could feel my pussy dripping and making my panties wetter and wetter.

He moaned into my mouth and it only made me want him more. I ran my hands along his face, caressing that beautifully shaped beard and down his neck. I wanted to feel his chest against my hands because his body was beautiful, even with the scars left by the bullets.

I pulled up his shirt and I got my wish. He let my lips go and sucked my breasts, sliding my panties to the side and pushing his fingers inside of my love. My head fell back in so much pleasure.

"Kol...please," I begged. He sucked harder and his thumb violently began to rub my clit.

My body responded to him like no one else. I shivered, rocking back and forth against his hands.

"Kol please stop playing with me!"

"Not yet, baby!" Kol yelled. Just when I was feeling close, right when I was about to release and drown my panties, Kol took his fingers out and put his mouth on my pussy!

He licked his tongue inside me and sucked hard on my clit in just enough time to catch my explosion all over his mouth.

"OH MY GOD, KOL! FUCK!" I yelled. I came so hard on his face. I was breathless, pulling his head farther into my love. He continued to lick and suck as I emptied myself into his mouth.

"Your pussy tastes so good to me, and I have missed it," Kol said.

Barely breathing, I begged, "Please, inside me now, Kol."

"This is what I was waiting for," Kol said. He pulled off his clothes and before I could finish convulsing, he was inside me.

Kol was fucking me so hard. He looked into my wide eyes and his beautiful hazel eyes were darker than normal.

"Baby I have missed your pussy so much!" Kol yelled.

"Please, Kol, I need you," I whispered into his ear. I was begging just like he said. "Kol!" My body was shivering, but I didn't want him to stop.

He flipped me over on top of him, and I slid on top of his dick. It was pure ecstasy, and I wanted to savor every piece of his dick slowly. I slammed down on it, gasping. He held onto my thigh with one hand, gripping it tighter while he sucked on my breast with pure aggression.

Oh Lord, trying to savor this dick was too hard. I rocked harder and faster, faster, and faster. I came so hard Heat pulsed through me. Kol thrusted into my love, bringing me back to life. Sitting up on chaise, he pumped harder and harder and harder. He held me to him, breathing, "Say you love me! Say you love me! Sam, say you love me!"

"I love you Kol," I said. "Oh my God, I LOVE YOU!"

Waking up had never felt so good. My body was still reeling from the night before. Small snippets of last night were etched into my thoughts, and it made me smile. I heard the shower running, and I realized I hadn't had my mouth on his dick last night.

I had neglected him. Since my hair was already a mess, I thought, *what the hell?* Waking up naked was an advantage. I opened the shower and stepped in.

"Good morning, Kol," I said.

"Good morning, Goddess," he replied. I immediately fell to my knees and slipped his dick into my mouth!

A deep groan came from his lips, and I smiled. I loved getting him off. It was hot, steamy, and intoxicating. When I popped my lips on his head, it drove him crazy. "Fuck," he said, and that was his undoing!

I was so glad Mom had agreed to keep Chase. We really needed that time together.

After I got into my car, the phone rang, and it was Tony.

"Look Sam," he said, "I know what I said. I was just pissed at you because I thought you had lost your edge. I know you have a kid now, and you need some time to focus. It's just not the you I remember, the girl I could get to do anything for me, the bitch I loved."

"Right, I'm not her," I said, "and I haven't been her for some time now. I left all of that behind, pushed it from my mind to move on with my life. I have a baby and a husband to think of."

"What, you got married overnight or something?"

"Tony, you know what I mean. Look, back to Alisha, where is she now?"

"She is still in Detroit, but she has gone to a shitty neighborhood. She is meeting with some messy ass people that will kill first. Look, I don't know if she is getting them for you or your *husband*."

"Either way, can I still count on you, Tony? Kol just got released from the hospital, and I don't want him getting hurt again."

"So, it's me that you need again, just like you use to."

"Tony, I don't want the extra sarcasm from you. I just need to know you have me if I need you."

"Baby, you always have me, whenever! I'll get with you later," he said before hanging up.

He sounded so weird. *Maybe Charese was right?* I asked myself. *She couldn't be. Tony couldn't possibly think there is a chance for him, could he?* I decided to call her later. I went to my mom's house to get Chase.

"Hey mom, look at my big man!" I greeted when I saw Chase. "Chase, Mommy and Daddy missed you."

"Look at him," my mom said. "I swear he gets more handsome by the day."

"Momma, you are just too much."

"I just love him so much, Sam."

"I know you do."

"When can I keep him again?"

"Really mom? He is still here, right in your arms. Kol only has one more appointment with Dr. Johnson, and if all goes well next week, we are clear to go back to Chicago."

"No sweetie, I have enjoyed having you around, especially Chase."

"I know, Mom."

"Sam, why don't I keep Chase this week, then I can get all the time I can before you take him away?"

"Mom, I would have to get his things over here, are you sure?"

"I am, and I bet you and Kol could use the alone time. He just got out of the hospital, take some time, and love on each other."

"I will need to run this by Kol; he hasn't really spent a lot of time with Chase."

"Why don't you call him and ask?" she suggested, so I did.

"Kol, hey baby," I said when he picked up.

"Hey, are you ok?" he asked.

"Yes, I'm fine."

"Where are you?"

"I am at Mom's; She wants to keep Chase for the week, so she can spend some time with him before we leave. Are you ok with that?"

"I mean, my little guy has been away from me, and I have missed him."

"I know, but Mom wants us to have some alone time before we go home," I said.

"In that case, I think we will be ok with that. As long as Mom knows we will be coming by every day, then it's ok with me."

"Are you sure, Kol?"

"Yes, Mom has been wonderful throughout all of this and a little time with Glam-ma won't hurt."

Chapter Twenty

"I would love to have more nights like last night," I said.

"Are you blushing, Sam?" Kol asked. "I will pack up some of Chase's things and bring them over."

"Are you sure you feel up to it?" I asked him.

"I am, and besides, I can see Mom," he answered. "Tell her I love her for this, and I will see you soon."

"I will."

Soon, Kol arrived and my mom, Chase, and I were all pleased to see him.

"Kol, look at you, son, you look great," said Mom.

"Hello, Mom, I have missed you. You know you don't have to keep Chase, we are fine with him."

"I know you are, but I want to be able to give you this time because you will be gone soon. I won't be able to see you every day."

"You mean, see Chase every day," I said. "Mom, we are just a few hours away."

"Yeah, we will see you all the time every holiday, birthdays, and not to mention, I want to marry your daughter as soon as possible."

"Well, son, when you put it that way, it eases my heart just a little more."

Mom," I said.

"Yes, Sam?" she answered.

"You are going overboard. Kol and I will send pictures to you weekly, and let's not forget about Facetime. We will see you at least once a week."

"I love you for this, Mom," Kol said, "and you are sure you can keep Chase?"

"Yes, you two go and have fun this last week. Once you get back to Chicago, it's all about Chase, and you two don't matter anymore!"

"Thanks Mom," Kol told her as I hugged her tight. "Call us if you need anything. Sam, I will meet you back at home, ok?"

"Yes, I have to just run an errand or two. Do you need me to bring anything home specific?"

"No, just you."

"Ok, I will see you soon."

A whole week without Chase, what would Kol and I do? I was going to make a run to the store and get some sensual things, so we can really enjoy this week.

Kol

I called Kevin as soon as I got to my car. "Hey, Kevin, yeah man, how is it going since you got out?" He asked.

"Good, did you work out everything with Sam?"

"Yes, I think after last night, I have her back on my side."

"Good, man, I am glad you squashed that shit!"

"I told Sam the truth about everything."

"I guess she didn't run, did she, Kol?"

"No, she didn't run."

"I told you, Kol. She is a ride or die chick, just like I thought she was."

"Look, while you are giving her the high praise, I still have someone on it."

"What the fuck, Kol? I thought you left the shit alone?"

"I can't, Kevin, she has done too much. I convinced Sam that it was over, and I wanted to help her, but I lied! I want to crush this bitch."

"Man, are you sure you want to do this? You are barely walking, and you want to go back on it?"

"Yes, Kevin, I do! I have someone dropping some info at the old spot. I have someone picking it up and will get it to me."

"Kol, what do you need me to do?"

"Nothing at all, just keep your head low, and if anything comes up there, let me know."

"I got you, bro."

"Look, take care and tell my girl I said what's up."

"Watch that shit, Kevin. You know how I am about my woman."

I hated lying to Sam, but that bitch, Alisha, was beyond help. She had already checked out of every facility she had checked into. She knew how to play the system, and that's why I knew she meant to do everything she said she would.

She was manipulative and could fool everyone else, but I knew better. I wouldn't give her the chance to strike again.

Now, I had to get to the store for some dinner. If I knew my sexy woman, she was getting everything else we needed to stay in the entire week. I better get enough food to get us through.

Sam

"Charese, hey are you home?" I asked over the phone. "I am running a few errands, and I want to stop by in about an hour or so? You have time to see me?"

"Yeah, sure, Sam."

"Thanks, see you then." When I got to Charese, she was so anxious to know what happened.

"Sam, what is going on?" she asked before I could make it through the door.

"Charese, this Tony shit is really bothering me."

"Where is Chase?"

"With Mom, she has kidnapped him for the week before we go back to Chicago."

"The doctor has released Kol?"

"Next week, if he is still in good working order, which he is from what I remember last night."

"You better take it easy on him."

"Whatever, I have missed him."

"TMI, Sam!"

"Look, I talked to Tony today, and it was definitely weird. He went off on me a few days ago, talking about me wanting to wait was not like the bitch he was in love with!"

"Ok Sam, did he say used to be in love with or is in love with. Be sure of what you are saying."

"He said in love with," I said.

"OH MY GOD!"

"I know. Charese, he can't mean it like that, could he? No way!"

"Sam, I told you what everyone thought. Everyone knew you were his, and he hated it when you went straight. There has always been talk that you would be back with him, that's why he never had a serious relationship. I mean, bitch, you never noticed?"

"No, Charese, I hadn't. When I left, I left and didn't look back. I never called, texted, or anything. I was so far from him."

"I don't know what you are going to do. I told your dumb ass not to open that door ever again and call him, didn't I?"

"Yes, I should have listened to you. I am just going to have to face him and tell him to leave it alone completely. That way, I won't have anything left to discuss. I will ask Kol if he can have his people stay on Alisha. He said he wanted to help her, and I believe him."

"You do? I don't know, Sam. If he was like you said he was back in the day, do you really think he could just let this go like this?"

"Well, that's what he told me. and I trust him. I need to tell Tony to just drop it. I will call him tomorrow and get it all worked out. I am not going to mess this evening up thinking about Tony. I am all about my man," I said.

When I got home, there was music, flowers, dinner, and him, only him. He had on jeans that hung just right, no socks, no shoes, no shirt, and only a dinner towel draped over his shoulder. He was so inviting with that dazzling smile as he looked at me.

"You, Kol Martin, are going to be the death of me," I said, "and I think it's going to be sooner than later."

We laughed through dinner and talked about our lives before each other.

It was all the fun stuff and none of the heavy stuff. It was nice just looking at him. His lack of a shirt and socks were making my body sing. I had to control myself and give him a break. He had put in so much work last night and this morning for me, I wanted him to just rest. I wanted to just enjoy being with Kol.

"It was really nice that your mom wanted to keep Chase for us," Kol said. "She is amazing."

"Of course, she is my mom," I said. Dinner was finished, and we wanted to just settle in. I decided on a movie and it was the classic, *Love Jones.* "Who doesn't love this movie?" I asked.

"What is it about *Love Jones* that people love so much?" Kol asked. I wanted to punch him!

"What the hell are you talking about? You've never seen this movie?" I asked.

"No, I never wanted to before."

"Well shit! I knew something was coming?"

"What are you talking about, Sam?"

"I knew there had to be at least one thing I didn't like about your perfect ass. This is the movie of all love movies! You, sir, are going to watch it, and you will enjoy it." He just laughed, and we started the movie. I noticed how he began changing as the movie went on.

He did really enjoy it, especially the scene with Charlie Parker. "Say, baby, can I be your slave?" Kol asked.

"I told you, this movie is for lovers," I said. "If you've ever been in love before, this movie says it all. It's like how you felt when you hear Lenny Williams' 'Because I love you.'" The atmosphere changed as we debated over the movie and the songs. We could feel the heat floating in the room.

Being without him for so long, I wanted to get my feel. I couldn't get enough of him. It was like I was waiting for the other shoe to drop, and if it did, I want to be there. As I stared into his beautiful hazel eyes, I knew what he was thinking. My pulse raced, and I knew he could see my heartbeat. I felt like it was about to jump out and run for its life.

As the credits still rolled, he kissed my cheek, slowly dragging his hands down my arm. I swear my body bent to this mans will. I was so sensitive to his touch.

"You are mine," he whispered in my ear. It was like a deeper side of him had reared!

"Yours?" I said.

"Yes, Sam, all mine and no one else's ever again." I switch the TV over to Pandora. The Brian McKnight station was on, playing "Love of My Life."

"I want you," Kol said. "Waking up to you every day isn't enough, Sam. Being with you every day isn't enough. You being the mother of my child isn't enough."

"What are you saying, Kol?"

"Let's get married now, as soon as possible. I need you to be mine. I need you to be Mrs. Kol Martin now. After the doctor releases me, we can get married then."

"Kol, that's in a week!"

"You would be surprised with what Candice can get done in a week," he said.

"Kol, we haven't decided on anything, not colors, a place, family, friends, a honeymoon!"

"I have been on my honeymoon since I met you, Sam."

"But Kol, I am only getting married once, and I want this to be my dream wedding."

"It can be Sam. I know we can make it happen. I want you to be my wife now, mine!"

I looked into his eyes and he meant it. He wanted to be my husband. With the realization, my body radiated with heat. Knowing that he had to have me, sent my body in pure overdrive!

"Kol, baby, yes. I will marry you next week! Hell, I will marry you tomorrow, and we can plan a reception later for all I care. I am ready to be completely yours," I said.

He pulled my lips to his, pushing my hands up to his face, and around his neck. He pulled me closer to him. My nipples hardened, and he found them immediately. How did he know just where to place his hands on my body? It was unbelievable! Releasing my mouth, Kol tugged at my ear with his teeth and cupped my breasts just right. They fit in his hands with just a little overflow. Trust me, my now-full C's love him.

His mouth was sucking, biting, and teasing me. I held my legs tightly together and it felt like my juices were going to flood my jeans. How could he do this to me? He was making me lose my inhibitions. He could ask me anything, and I wouldn't deny him. He could touch me anywhere, mark me as his!

I saw myself doing things for him I would never do for anyone else. Kol brought out an inner freak in me that I didn't know was there. I wanted to please him in every way, and I really meant in EVERY WAY!

Later on, at Kol's doctor's appointment...

Kol

"Dr. Johnson, it's good news, right?" I asked.

"Yes, Mr. Martin, it's great news," said the doctor. "You have completely healed, and there is no reason not to release you. With that being said, continue taking care of yourself. Exercise regularly and continue to eat right. It's time to get back to your lives. Ms. Smith is taking great care of you, and I recommend you keep allowing her too."

"We can't thank you enough Dr. Johnson," I said.

"Oh, you are invited to our wedding too," Sam added. "You helped us get to this day."

"Wonderful, when is it?"

"Since you've released me, it'll be in about a week. I will send you the details," I said.

"A week, that's fast!" Dr. Johnson remarked.

"Well, Doctor, when you have what I have with Sam, especially with everything that's happened, you just don't want to lose any more time. I have got to marry her!"

Later on, I called Candice.

"Hey, Candice, what's up girl?" I greeted.

"Nothing, Kol, what did the doctor say?" my sister asked.

"He said I'm good and completely healthy, so Sam and I need a favor."

"Anything. I am so glad you are ok. Mom has been going crazy waiting to hear from you two."

"Well, tell her this! You have a little over a week to pull off our wedding."

"What?"

"Sam and I have decided not to wait, and I need you to do your thing. We want to get married now, next Saturday to be exact," I told her.

"Jesus Christ, Kol, how am I going to do that?" she asked. "Never mind," she answered herself. "I just need where, time, colors, and a guest list with numbers, emails, or whatever you have."

"We don't have much," I said.

"Oh God, I am about to die! I can only pull this off if there are no additional parties to take care of, which means, no bridesmaids, no best men, and no ring bearers. It will just be you two and the minister standing. Will that be ok with Sam?"

"Yes, Candice, that will be just fine," Sam said. "I love you brother and will do anything to become his right now."

"Ok good, I am ready to work. I need to know do you want to get married and have the reception at the same place or travel between places?"

"All in one if it's possible."

"Ok great, and what kind of food do you want? Full meals or just typical wedding food?"

"You decide, Candice. "We don't care about that," I said.

"Are you sure, Kol?" She asked.

"Yes, but we do care about the music. I want David Ruffin, Earth, Wind, and Fire, Frankie Beverly and Maze, and Charlie

Parker! I want music that means something!" Old school all the way.

"No problem, I got it," said Candice.

"Kol, what do you want?"

"I just want Sam, everything else is just extra," I answered.

"Candice, we want a classic black with a red and pink color scheme," Well that's Sam said. "Whatever and however you pull it off is up to you."

. "Ok, how many people do you expect?"

"It will be such short notice, but let's plan for at least 200 people," I said.

"Kol, are you serious?"

Candice answered, "Kol Martin is being taken off the market completely. Trust me, everyone will want to be at this one. Ok, and the cake? Any particular flavors?"

"No, you have complete control," I told her. "We have given you our most important points, and you have the reigns from here."

"Are you sure?" Candice asked.

"Yes!"

"Ok, do you want to call Mom now, or do you want me to tell her?"

"No, Candy, this is our news to tell. We'll tell our moms first, and then, we will let you know when you can start the snow storm."

Sam

"Hey Mom, what are you doing?" I asked once she picked up.

"Nothing; are you and Kol enjoying your time together?" she asked.

"Yes, Mom, can you hold on a second?" I asked and gave Kol the phone.

"Sure."

"Mom are you there?"

"Yes, Kol, how are you and the family?"

"Fine, Mom, look I need to conference another call in, ok?" He dialed his mom's number, while my mom waited quietly.

"Mom?" he said once he thought they both picked up.

"Yes," they both answered in unison.

"Kol and I have you both on the line," I said. "Something has happened."

"OH, MY GOD, it's not Alisha again?" my mom asked.

"Are you two okay?" Kol's mom asked.

"Yes, it's nothing like that. Please calm down," Kol said.

"Will one of you tell us what is going on?" my mom asked.

"Moms, we have decided to get married next Saturday," I said.

"What?" the both asked.

"Yes, my jet will bring you and the family from Chicago on Friday morning," said Kol. "I'll book the rooms for you guys, and everything else has been taken care of."

"Candy has started working on everything already," I said.

"Christ, Sam, are you serious?" my mom asked.

"Yes, waiting months to marry this man is too long," I answered.

"We have been through so much and waiting just isn't an option anymore," Kol said. "We hope you two are okay with this."

"Nell, what do you think?" my mom asked.

"Lue, I think it's great, and I can't wait!" said Kol's mom.

"Me either!" said my mom.

"Well, the hard work has been done. Now for the fun part!" Let's call Candice!

"Candy, you can spread the word now."

"You will wed at the Botanic Gardens on Saturday at 7:00 pm. I am sending over the layout for you to approve right now!"

Chapter Twenty-One

"Oh, my goodness," I exclaimed. "This is breathtaking! Candice, how did you do this and so fast? Approved? Everything? Now, I have work to do."

"I told you, Sam, she is the best at this stuff," Kol said.

"Ok, great," Candice said. "Now, time for the most important thing."

"What, the dress?" I asked.

"No, I am about to tweet, Instagram, snapchat, and Facebook the announcement! Get ready, Sam. You, my dear, are about to go viral!" she squealed.

The post read: *One of Chicago's most eligible bachelors is calling it quits. He is marrying the beautiful Samantha Smith on Saturday in Memphis, TN. This picture says it all! #KolandSamanthaforever!*

"Oh God, Charese and the girls are going to freak," I said. "I better call them now." I was too late; however, my phone was already ringing.

"Sam!" Charese yelled. How in the fuck do you tell the entire world before us?"

"I was about to call. I didn't know it was going out so fast, I promise. I know you are upset, but this is so about Kol and I, not anyone else. We deserve this, especially after everything we have been through. Can you all just be happy for us, and we will talk about everything else later, ok?"

"Alright, Sam," Charese said. "Congratulations!"

"Thank you! I love you guys, you know that, but I have to do this. He is mine, and I am his and that's all that matters now." Candice sure knew how to make an announcement!

"Look at this, Kol," I said, showing him the status and all the comments.

Kol Martin and Sam Smith will be officially married in 8 days! Candice's next post read. *I love my brother and my new sister is freaking incredible. Love has conquered all.* #myfamily #bonded #offthemarket

"Shit," I said, "it has been retweeted so many times! Good grief, social media is having a field day with this one."

"Sam, I told you that you were getting the best and the world seems to agree," said Kol.

"Kol, you know if this has gone viral, Alisha knows and will come here. I'm going to have to kill her on our wedding day."

"Don't worry your pretty little head! I will have plenty of security. If she comes within 50 miles of here, she will be taken care of."

"Baby, I don't want to worry about Alisha, this is about us. You are certain you can do this, really sure?"

"Sam, trust me, you and Chase are my priority. Alisha will not get close to my family. I am committed to you, and I won't let anything, or anyone destroy our wedding day. You have made me the happiest man in the world. We have eight days and counting. Let's make it an awesome eight days!" Kol exclaimed.

"Honeymoon! Kol, we need talk to Candy about the honeymoon," I said.

"We are going a few places," Kol said. "I have a boat ready to take us wherever you want to go, Mrs. Martin. We will be leaving from New Orleans on Sunday. Saturday night we will stay at the Peabody, train ride to New Orleans on Sunday Morning, and we leave port whenever you desire."

"I love you, Kol," I said excitedly.

"I love you, Sam, today, tomorrow, and forever!" Kol said and kissed me. "Hey, I have a few things to take care of for the wedding. I'll see you later, babe."

"Okay, my love," I said, as he left.

Now, there was just one thing I had to take care of myself. I called Tony.

"Hey, Tony?" I said when he answered.

"Yea, so congratulations are in order, right? In 7 days, you will be officially married?" he asked.

"That's why I called. I wanted to tell you to let it go. I don't want to be consumed by Alisha anymore, and I believe Kol will take care of it. I want to thank you for having my back, Tony, but it's over now. I wanted to say thanks for being my friend." It was silent for a moment. "Tony, are you still there?"

"Yea, I'm here," he answered. "So, that's it? It's over just like that?"

"I mean, Tony, I don't know what else you want me to say."

"You know, Sam, you have always been perceptive and smart. How can you just call me and say this shit to me, to me of all people?"

"What are you talking about, Tony?" I asked.

"Sam, I was willing to kill for you. I was willing to take care of what your man wouldn't. Alisha is no longer a problem! Your soon-to-be husband waited too long. I already had the bitch axed," he said.

"Wait, what? Tony, what have you done?"

"When she found out about the wedding yesterday, the bitch went crazy and contacted the screwball crew I told you about. It wasn't Kol she wanted to kill, just like I thought, it was you and your baby."

"I can't believe this!"

"Well, believe it! She put a hit out on you, and I just couldn't stand back and do nothing! Your man got the word this morning., and he didn't say anything. Well fuck that! I wasn't about to play with the life of the woman I love like that."

"What did you just say, Tony?" I asked.

"You heard me, Sam, I love you! I always have and always will."

"Tony, you don't –"

"I wasn't about to stand by and watch that bitch have you killed, so I had to get to her. She only paid the crew some of the cash, and when she was dealt with, no one was around to pay the rest, so they just dropped it. It was easy to get to her too. Since she'd been so erratic lately, no one doubted that she killed herself. They found her in the same hotel where she killed her family. It was fucking epic."

"Tony! You didn't do this?" I asked.

"Are you fucking kidding me right now, Sam? This bitch was about to take you out. What did you expect me to do?"

"Talk to me, Tony. Kol and I could've handled it our way."

"Fuck that, Sam, I want you, and your fuck boy will just have to deal with it! You won't be getting married Saturday to him or anybody else. You are mine now, always have been and always will be. I am coming to get you and the kid, so be ready!"

"Tony! No! I won't leave him, and I won't be with you!"

"What the fuck did you say?" he asked.

"Ok, Tony so this is what you've wanted all along, haven't you? You wanted to be my motherfucking hero! You wanted to take care of things, so I would swoon over you like a little lost puppy!" Well, I am so sorry for you," I told Tony. "You got me so fucked up, boy! See, the bitch in me hasn't been out in quite some time, but she is still in charge, calling all the fucking shots. I have tolerated your shit this whole time. Charese warned you still had a thing for me. You're pathetic, fucking pathetic! You try that shit, and your body will be the one they find next."

"Are you threatening me, Sam," Tony asked.

"Tony, I was taught by the best, and that was you. Come near me or my family if you want to and find out what you and Alisha have in common. It's the afterlife! Don't ever contact me again. I will forget this conversation ever happened, and we both can move on."

"Move on? Sam, you could never move on from me."

"Tony, at one point in life I trusted you, and for you to come at me like this, it hurts the shit out of me! I can push that to the side, though, if you really want to threaten my baby, my husband, or me!"

"Ok Sam, you want this shit to be war?"

"I will fight your ass to the death!"

"No, I wouldn't dream of hurting you," he answered, "but that motherfucker has this hold on you. He's got to go."

"What are you talking about, Tony?"

"Yea, I know he left to take care of stuff for this wedding that won't happen. Just look outside! I have been waiting to come in there and take you away. Open the fucking door, Sam, NOW!"

I hung up the phone and yelled, "It's open, Tony. Now what? You know I am not afraid of you, don't you?"

"Yes, I am well aware, and that's one of the reasons I love you so much," Tony said, walking into my home.

"Tony, do you even know what love is?" I asked, trying to hide how shocked I was. "The shit you are feeling isn't love, it's envy, motherfucker! You hate not having what you want and that's it. You haven't loved me ever! If you did, you wouldn't be doing this now. Tony, this shit has been over for a lifetime, and you know it. Except it and let go."

"Sam?"

"What, Tony?"

"Somewhere in there, Sam, I know you still love me. You just need time to remember it."

"Tony, what the hell happened to you? I have never heard you talk about love. You told me once a year you loved me. That's why it was so easy to walk away from you."

"Well, you were wrong, Sam. You changed my heart, and I love the shit out of you."

"I don't believe you. When have you ever showed it to me."

"I couldn't show it. I couldn't wear my love for you on my sleeve out in the open. How would that look? Me in love? People would try to use you against me. Who would fear me or take me seriously? But remember, when we made love? Remember how I held you, kissed you, and tasted you. I know you felt it then. How close I felt to you. You had to know how much I loved you, bitch! Sam, you had me wrapped around your finger. I put people on this fool for you, Sam, no other reason. Do you think anyone else I used to fuck could call me and ask me for the shit you did? No, because I don't love them. I love you, Sam!"

"Stop it, Tony, just stop it. I am done, and I won't continue this conversation or whatever the hell this is. Just get the hell out of my house. Never cross me again or you will regret it!" I yelled. I walked over to the front door and flung it open. Kol stood in the doorway.

"Hey baby, this is…" I started.

"I know who it is," Kol said. "His name is Tony. He is the one who ordered the hit on Alisha."

"Kol, baby, how did you know?" I asked.

"Baby, I am good at my job for a reason. Oh Tony, just so you know, all your boys are gone too," Kol said.

"What the hell?" Tony started.

"Don't worry, they're not dead… yet. But that's not a problem. See, you did your research, but you found out what I wanted you to."

"Kol!" I cried.

"Sam, not now," he said, and his voice roared at me. He turned on Tony. "I let you get what you wanted, and I have been watching your moves ever since, all your contact with my wife, tracking me with I went back to Chicago. I know your every move. Your gang isn't as loyal as you think. There are always leaks, and I am good at takeovers. You have a choice, Tony. You can stay here, do what you do, and never contact my wife again, or you can take your chances. What option do you choose?"

"Fuck you, Kol, you're nothing and you can't touch me," Tony replied.

"Is that what you really think? I can't touch you? Which place will you run to tonight? Your normal place in the north, and by the way; it's too accessible. What about your pad in South Memphis, Millington, or the legit house in Lions Gate in the haven? See, I know every hole you have, even the ones you tell your mother to run to when it gets hot!

"See, to be me, you have to be a motherfucker, and I am. Your baby and the bitch you tell every day you love her, I know everything, and I mean everything. I am not to be fucked with when it comes to Sam! Everything you have a hand in, I know about it."

"So, you know a few things about me, and you think that scares me?" Kol asked.

"I am fucking Tony Hunter!"

"Well, Mr. Hunter, you can walk out of my house on your own or be taken out! What's your choice?"

"Damn, Sam, I underestimated your fuck boy! He has some balls on him. You always did like big balls, I should know."

"Tony, get out of my life for good," I yelled. "And if you show up at my wedding on Saturday, I will shoot you myself!"

"I'll go for now, but on Saturday, you will be waiting for me and not him," Tony said, turning away. Kol lunged for him, but I grabbed his arm.

"Kol, baby, don't! He is nothing. He is barely holding on. He has nothing. He is one move away from being put in for life. He has one more time, and it's over. He won't jeopardize that for anyone, not even me," I said. I turned back to Tony. "Leave now, Tony, while you still can."

"Have fun tonight with her, Kol," said Tony, "because this is the last time you will be left alone with my woman!"

"That's it –" Kol started. I lunged for Tony. "Sam no!"

"Bitch, you tried to cut me!" Tony yelled, grabbing me by my neck.

"Tony, let her go!" Kol yelled. "Take your hands off her now!

"I knew she always wanted my hands back around her throat," said Tony. "She used to like that."

"Tony, if you hurt one hair on her head –"

"What, Kol? What can you do other than shut the fuck up? I told you I would have you soon. Haven't I always done just what I told you, Sam? I hate you are making me do this, but I have no choice. I feel threatened. I feel my life is in danger."

"Tony, just let me go, and we can forget all of this. If you stop now, I will go with you!"

Sam, what the hell?"

"No, Kol, I love you too much! I won't put you in danger. Chase needs you!"

"I am doing this all for you, baby, because I love you."

"Kol, just walk away. Get Chase and go back to Chicago," I told him.

"Listen to her, Kol! She is right," Tony said. "I will kill you where you stand, and she know me, better than anyone."

Chapter Twenty-Two

"Tony, look, I said I will go with you. Just give me a minute to say goodbye to him. He deserves that from me," I said.

"He deserves nothing, Sam!" Tony yelled.

"Please, Tony! I am already going, so just give me this. Kol, I love you with all I am. I have never loved anyone like you before. My soul feels you daily. My heart smiles at the thought of you. I see your love in skylines, in sound, breezes, and color. You, Kol Martin, are the love of my life, and I will gladly hang onto the memories of us if it will keep you and Chase safe. I will let you go and suffer, but what I won't do is allow you to feel any pain, remember? Remember what I said back in the club in Chicago? I will feel it for you," I told him.

"Sam, I can't let you do this," Kol said.

"Can you two wrap this shit up?" Tony interrupted.

"Fuck you, Tony! You want me to go with you, then let me say goodbye my way," I replied and turned back to Kol. "Kol, I love you today, tomorrow, and forever. Hold me close for the last time, be close to me one more time. I need this to move on without you." With tears rolling down my face, I whispered to him, "If I don't make it, take care of our son and know I had no choice.

"Sam, no!" Kol yelled.

"Just kiss me you fool," I whispered. "Please Kol!" I felt his hurt, almost as if it was a betrayal.

"That's enough," Tony shouted. "Enough!"

I could hear his footsteps coming towards us. He grabbed my arm and pulled me to him. Before I could talk myself out of it, I stabbed him in his chest with the letter opener. I had pulled it from the desk where Kol was standing. I turned it, so the wound wouldn't close. I wanted Tony to bleed out right there on my floor.

"Tony, I told you, I would kill you if you tried to hurt him, hurt us!" I said.

"Sam, you bitch," Tony said.

Kol pushed the letter opener in further, killing him. When the police arrive, I shook and cried in Kol's arms. They took my statement, and Kol and I were free to go.

It was over! Alisha and Tony were over! Finally, we could move on with our lives without having to look over our shoulders! It was finally over!

…….……..Five days later

"You have chosen to write your own vows," the minister said. "Sam, you may recite your vows."

"My love," I said, "I will now and forever be bonded to you. My life is forever entwined with yours. I promise to spend every waking moment making you happy, and the moments I am sleeping, I will be dreaming of it. I will love you through it all. I know that some days will be harder than others, but no matter what, I will always love you, cherish you, and forsake all

231

others for you. You are the light that beams inside my heart that makes every day worthwhile. I will love and honor you for the rest of our lives, and even after that. Now and forever, I am yours and you are mine."

"Kol, you may now recite your vows," Said the minister.

"From the day I looked into your eyes," Kol began, "I have been waiting on the day I could make you mine forever. I waited for you, for this happiness I feel right now. I knew that you being in my life for the rest of our days was a gift I didn't deserve. I am not worthy of your love, but because of your heart, you have chosen to let me in anyway. My love for you is strong, everlasting, and never ending. I will always be here to take care of you, protect you, and give you everything you deserve and more. You are my life force, and without you, I am nothing. Loving you is my life's pleasure. I will spend every day I have breath in my body making you happy. I love you, Sam, today, tomorrow, and forever."

Tears fell as I took at this man, breathing in his love, and I couldn't believe he is mine. The minister asked for the rings as I look into Kol's eyes.

Chase was the lucky guy we both trusted to hold them, in a case so he wouldn't eat them!

"With this ring, I thee wed," said Kol, sliding it on my finger more tears of joy fell.

"You may now kiss your bride," the minister said. Kol took me in entirely for I don't know or how long before we broke apart. "I have the pleasure of introducing you to for the first time, Mr. and Mrs. Kol Martin!" the minister exclaimed.

We took our son and walked down the aisle. Kol's arm was around me, and Chase was in my arms, smiling at all the streamers and balloons falling. Happiness is all I feel now! Pure bliss! We sat and watched our loved ones as they smiled and celebrated with us on this day. Our son, who we almost lost, bounced on my lap.

Kol was next to me. Our family and friends were gathered in one room to celebrate our love today. As I looked into Kol's eyes, and back to the crowed room, I saw love. Our first dance was to Charlie Parker's "Parker's Mood," the song that was on the *Love Jones* soundtrack. The song was the obvious choice for us.

Epilogue

It had been five years since that fateful day when Tony took his last breath on our floor. He bled out right there and was already dead when the police arrived. They had been trying to get him for years. I had been smart enough to record the part when he said that he loved me and didn't want Alisha to hurt me, so he took care of her. It was an open and shut case.

Kol and I have been happy ever since. Chase has grown so much and because of what we went through, Kol and I have an even stronger bond.

Everything about our lives has intensified. I am now in the family business. I help with all the marketing and promotions for the shops. Our business is up and growing too. We opened a new consulting firm and started a foundation for the mentally ill.

Kol is thriving at work. He is now the regional manager and the company is continuing to move in new areas of the world. We are truly blessed. The fact that my family doesn't have to look over our shoulders is wonderful. All of Tony's old connections have disappeared, and our lives have been quiet.

"Okay, Chase," I called. "Daddy is coming home today! I need you to be a good boy, ok? When the sitter comes, you have to be a good boy then, too." My son looked up at me with eager eyes and Kol's beautiful smile spread across his face. "We will only be gone overnight, but today, we can have all the fun we want with Daddy!" I told my son. "Look Chase, it's Daddy!" Chase ran to his father, laughing with his arms out.

Kol picked him up; my two boys walk towards me, and I have everything. Soon, the sitter arrives, and Kol and I are off on our date.

Kol booked that same suite as the one I stayed in the first time I visited him. The room was filled with all of the same things, but this time, he has added chocolate and strawberries.

"Sam, this is for you." Kol always gives me the best gifts, and as always, he doesn't disappoint.

"Kol, are we even leaving this room tonight? I mean, if we don't, I won't be disappointed."

"Sam, we can do anything you want. I want you to be happy, and if it makes you happy to be here with me, then that's what we will do."

"You are so easy, Kol."

"I want to give you my gift first, Sam. Is that okay this year?"

"Yes, my love, what is it?"

"While I was away, all I could think about was you and Chase, and how much I loved you both so much. So, I got you this."

"You got me an envelope?" I asked, jokingly.

"Baby, it's what's inside the envelope that's the gift," Kol said.

I opened it to reveal a deed.

"Kol, you bought me an island in fucking Brazil?"

"I hope you like it. I have the links and code for you to see everything, and we are going there in two weeks with everyone we love. Happy anniversary, baby!"

"Kol Martin, you have outdone yourself. I don't quite know if my gift will even measure up."

"You already gave me the best gift I could ask for: you. Chase was a bonus! I have everything I need. You don't ever have to give me another thing, Sam. What you have given me is enough."

"Ok then, I guess you don't need to know I am pregnant with baby number two!"

"You're pregnant?"

"Yes, Kol, I am having your baby again!"

"Sam, I love you... today, tomorrow, and forever!"

Back in Memphis...

"It's been five years since that bitch killed you, Tony. I hope the happy couple enjoyed their time together, brother, because it is about to come to an end."

.

CPSIA information can be obtained
at www.ICGtesting.com
Printed in the USA
BVHW032021230722
642785BV00019B/836

9 781724 233783